Free to Love

Sydell Lowell Voeller

Published by Sydell Voeller, 2023.

FREE TO LOVE

First edition. September 20, 2023.

ISBN: 979-8215946435

Written by Sydell Lowell Voeller.

Chapter One

"Oh no," Joanna Sullivan exclaimed under her breath. "If I don't get help, you're going to die." She peered anxiously at the brownish-black sea lion. Cutting into its neck was a blue nylon net.

What should she do? And *how*? This was an injured wild anima, not a household pet. Even though she'd been a state park ranger for over two years, that didn't qualify her to handle this alone.

The late September rain smarted against her face as she sprinted back up the empty beach, her mind racing. Normally this stretch was packed with tourists and weekenders, but now it appeared there was no one to help her.

Unexpectedly, an idea struck. Just that morning, on her way down the coast highway to the title company, she'd noticed a wildlife rehabilitation center—Anchorhold, the sign had read. Her only hope was to hurry back to her duplex and phone them.

Sidestepping a pile of driftwood, she hurried on until she came to the winding trail that led up from the beach. How long had the sea lion been trapped like this, she wondered anxiously. How many others were at risk?

At the top of the trail, she crossed a narrow strip of wild beach grass that led to her duplex. Its weathered gray shingles seemed to meld into the mist and the fog.

"Jo! Is that you?"

She looked up, stopping abruptly. She could barely detect the outline of a tall, broad-framed man who was waving to get her attention. Whoever it was, his voice sounded familiar. Apparently he'd arrived in the forest-green Jeep she saw parked behind her car in the driveway.

She approached cautiously, closing the distance between them. The man was wearing a navy-blue windbreaker, faded jeans, and a blue and white baseball cap.

Sudden recognition spiraled with confusion. "Austin!" she gasped. She caught her breath, a sharp stinging draft of air. For a paralyzing second she could have sworn it was Kyle her husband. But no, she reminded herself with a new rush of pain. Kyle was dead. She'd never see him again.

"Joanna Sullivan! What are you doing out here in this downpour?" he said gruffly, though his teasing grin grew wider with each passing second. "You'll catch your death of pneumonia!"

"I . . . I was out for an afternoon run." She pointed frantically back to the beach. There's a sea lion . . . not far from the bottom of the trail. It's got a fishing net caught around its throat. We've got to do something!"

His face registered alarm, instantly wiping away his grin. "Hold on! I'll go get the fishnet in my Jeep."

She heaved a sigh as she watched him hurry back to his Jeep. What was Austin, her former brother-in-law, doing here? How had he found her? Was this a spur-of-the-moment visit, perhaps? Or was he the bearer of *more* bad news? Hopefully it wasn't one of his parents, she thought her stomach churning. After Kyle had died, Ralph and Linetta Sullivan had set out for Africa to volunteer with the Peace Corps—the best way they knew to handle their grief.

Soon Austin returned with leather gauntlets and a wadded-up net about the size of a bedspread. "Let's try this," he said.

A few minutes later they were back on the beach, several yards away from the sea lion.

"Wait here," Austin whispered as he crept forward. In one swift motion, he crouched, threw the net snugly over the animal and dropped to his knees.

Joanna drew closer, hunching down too. "Hmm, pretty good size," she mused out loud. "A stellar sea lion, about fifty or sixty pounds." A raindrop trickled down her cheek and she backhanded it away.

Narrowing her gaze in concentration, she watched Austin whittle through the outer net with his Swiss army knife.

"Yeah, fifty or sixty pounds that would love to take a nip out of my hand," he said dryly. "Good thing I had this net. If I remember correctly, the closest tackle shop is almost an hour away." The knife pierced through the corded nylon. "Any wildlife clinics around here?" he asked.

"Uh-huh. Anchorhold. I was hurrying back to the house to call them when I saw you."

"Good. This fella needs antibiotics and observation." With deft movements, Austin carefully eased away the net that was piercing the sea lion's flesh.

While Austin worked, Joanna's gaze drifted to his hands. Large, masculine hands, tanned and strong. Hands so competent and agile. If anyone could handle this emergency, it would undoubtedly be Austin Sullivan. Judging from Kyle's boasting about him, Austin was one of the best veterinarians the San Francisco Zoo had ever known. But what was he doing here in Oregon? she wondered again.

"Hmm. Just what I was afraid of," he observed. "That wound is deep and there's purulent drainage."

"Most likely the work of a careless fisherman," Joanna said, indignation fringing her words. She straightened, propping her hands on her hips. "Now what? Shall I still call Anchorhold to come and get him, or should we try it ourselves?"

"I think we can do it. The less time we waste, the better. Let's roll up both ends of the fishnet like a hammock. Good thing the trail's not too steep."

In no time they'd hefted the sea lion in the back of the Jeep and were on their way to the wildlife center. As one mile gave way to the next, they talked companionably. He told her how he'd taken leave of absence from his job at the zoo. She told him how she'd accepted a position as a field guide at the Southport Aquarium about five miles down the coast highway. Her new assignment was in marked contrast to her former job as a state park ranger in the high desert of central Oregon. "Tomorrow will be my first day," she added.

"What'll you be doing there?"

"Mostly conducting public tours to coastal wetlands and estuaries. Two Capes State Park is right next to the aquarium, so the majority of the visitors come from the campgrounds. At the aquarium itself, I'll be narrating the nature shows."

They fell silent as they neared town. Through the rain-streaked windshield, she spied a kite shop on the right with a colorful array of wind socks and kites flapping in the wind.

"So you missed living on the coast these past few years," Austin said at last. His words were clearly a declaration, not a question.

"Yes. Dreadfully." She could hear the sea lion making thumping sounds in the bed of the pickup and reassured herself the drive to the wildlife center would soon be over. "When I was a little girl growing up almost fifty miles south of here, I spent lots of time, summers and winters both, beachcombing and exploring the tide pools." She smiled wanly. Funny how coming of age and the reality of loss had cast a shadowy pall on all that had once been special.

His voice was honey smooth. "Kyle used to tell me how you were always carting home injured seabirds, too."

Sudden recollection made her smile. "Uh-huh. Poor Mom. I can understand now how I must've driven her crazy."

He kept his eyes fixed on the highway ahead. "Kyle would be happy for you. He always wanted to take you back here some day. Some day after he'd become a more experienced fire fighter and could better pick and choose where he'd settle down."

Remembering, too, she swallowed the lump in her throat and stared out her side window. Groves of red-barked Madonna tress, intermingled with towering maples, whizzed by. "Yes, we did talk about that," she said softly. "We talked about that a lot. We planned to raise our kids in a small beach town a lot like Southport, a place where I could put my degree in environmental studies to good use. And at least here I have one relative close by, Aunt Marcella. We've stayed in close touch through e-mails and phone calls."

"Nice that you can have some family in town."

"Yes. When my sister, Stacey, and I were little girls, she and Uncle Ben used to visit often, always bringing us boxes of Cracker Jack or home-baked goodies." Joanna wanted to add more, to explain how it was her grief that had really fueled her move, not mere longing, nor convenience. But she knew she mustn't. It was much too soon to share such confidences even if he might still consider himself her brother-in-law.

The sign to Anchorhold loomed up ahead.

Minutes later, Dr. Ted Ashelman, the veterinarian on staff, greeted them warmly while three interns carted the sea lion onto an examination table.

"Can we help?" Austin asked after he'd introduced first Joanna, then himself. He handed the vet his business card.

The portly, white-haired veterinarian smiled his appreciation. "Yes, thanks. Just call me Ted. You might stand by while I administer a sedative, irrigate the wound, and give this critter an antibiotic."

"Glad to," Austin replied. He wrinkled his nose against the foul odor that mingled with the clinical smells of medicine and disinfectant. The sea lion, still mummied inside the fishing net, struggled beneath his restraining grasp. "Staph infection, I bet," he added.

Dr. Ashelman nodded as he opened a package of sterile gloves. "I'm afraid so. Less than an hour ago," he continued, "another couple brought in two injured seabirds with a fishhook embedded in their sides and a sandpiper caught in a strapping band."

Joanna bit her lip as new concern washed over her. Concern for the innocent wildlife. Concern for all God's creatures. Yes, something stirred deep inside of her again. Something long forgotten in the wake of her grief.

Fleetingly, her eyes met Austin's for some confirmation that he might be feeling the same way too.

His expression remained closed.

Yet how could he understand? she reasoned. He was a zoo vet—not a wildlife rehabilitator.

"Do you take in primarily birds?" Joanna asked while the older veterinarian drew up the medication in a plastic syringe and gave the injection.

"Yes, though we see other animals too. Many have been hit by cars, shot, ripped by barbed wire—you name it. Some can be treated and released immediately. But many others, like our friend right here, require a longer stay. Still others, the young and orphaned, need careful nurturing. To us, no animal is too small or insignificant. They all receive the same diligent care."

"But it's got to be tough," Austin interjected. "Tough to know exactly how to treat a wild animal when there's limited, if any established standards."

Dr. Ashelman adjusted the exam light above the table to get a better look at the now sedated sea lion. "Right. Wildlife rehab is still such a fledgling science. Most of my colleagues, especially those from veterinary school, have gone into domestic animal practice. The need for research and research workers is growing by leaps and bounds." With his gloved hands and squares of sterile gauze, he expressed the drainage, then began flushing out the wound.

Half an hour later, after the sea lion had been transported to the recovery unit, Dr. Ashelman agreed to Joanna's request for a quick tour of the rehab clinic.

She soon discovered that a variety of marine wildlife, in an assortment of sizes, shapes, and species, filled every nook and cranny. The very young, lacking fur or feathers, were lying under heat lamps, eyes tightly closed, while others were cocooned in flannel or wool scraps warmed by heating pads. Most were housed in assorted wire cages, both inside and out. In a large rectangular aquarium-sized outdoor pool swam another recovering sea lion.

They watched a volunteer feeding a baby squirrel through a minuscule plastic tube. They passed by two abandoned baby eagles that had been discovered by sky divers and rushed to the clinic. They saw a young raccoon that had injured its foot in a trap, an orphaned fawn, an owl that had been hit by a pickup while swooping onto the highway one night to catch a rat. The list seemed to go on and on.

"How many new animals do you take in on an average day?" Joanna asked, wondering how so few staff could handle the work. All the while, her awareness of Austin standing close beside her was growing crazily. She was thankful for a reason, at least for the time being, to keep her attention focused on what the vet was saying. But it wasn't easy.

"We take in an average of perhaps a dozen or so new animals," Ted Ashelman replied,. "But we've been known to see as many as sixty. Fortunately, more and more people are starting to hear about Anchorhold and rallying to the aid of the injured and orphaned. The baby eagles we visited a short while ago were flown in on a private jet by the sky divers who found them."

After exchanging good-byes with the veterinarian and the rest of the staff, and acknowledging their invitation to drop in to visit any time, Joanna and Austin started back for the duplex. It was nearly dusk. The wind had risen. The windshield wipers hummed while rain drops drummed against the roof of the Jeep. As the highway twisted and turned paralleling the ocean, the silence hung between them.

Joanna stared down at the tumultuous expanse of gray-blue water. High waves crashed against rocky cliffs, spewing up fountains of sea spray that dissipated into the nebulous gray mist.

Her stomach knotted as she pulled her gaze away. The turbulent water below seemed to underscore the upheaval growing inside of her.

The beached sea lion . . . Austin's unannounced appearance . . . the new insights she'd gleaned at Anchorhold . . . yes, it was all so sudden, and she wasn't sure what to make of it. But one thing she *did* know for certain. No matter how numb she felt, no matter how much she'd mourned for Kyle, she couldn't afford to simply stop caring about the wildlife she loved.

Later, back at the duplex, Joanna and Austin sat on the carpet in front of a roaring fire, their backs against the couch while they sipped steaming cups of coffee and talked. Outside, the wind and rain rattled the windows. Inside, the fire warmed them, sputtering and crackling as it sent forth the sweet smells of apple wood. The steady *ping, ping,* of rainwater striking the inside of an aluminum bucket sounded from the corner of the room.

Somehow it all felt so familiar, *too* familiar. Being with Kyle like this at the end of each day had always given her reassurance, an innermost resolve that as long as she was his wife, nothing could be too difficult to bear.

She gave a quick shake of her head, reminding herself that the man next to her was Austin, not Kyle. Truth was, she barely knew him. Austin had been Kyle's best man for their wedding, rushed back eighteen months later to help her lay Kyle to rest, and phoned a few times afterwards. Aside from that, he was almost a stranger.

Austin rose slowly, stretching out to his full six-and-a-half-feet, then crossed the room to toss another log on the fire. "So do you always up and move without telling anyone?" he asked, his back still turned to her.

"I really did intend to try to contact you." She paused to take a sip of coffee. "I've only been here a couple of weeks." It was true. She hadn't intended to hide from anyone, not for long, at least. Still, she hadn't bargained for this unexpected visit.

***

He turned to face her again. "No big deal, Jo. I'm not the world's best when it comes to staying in touch myself."

How could he blame her? he reminded himself, especially when part of this was his fault. He should've called her more often, at least made an attempt to e-mail or text her. Most of all, he should've scheduled his leave a few weeks earlier in order to help her. But he hadn't.

He glanced about at the disarray of moving crates, unpacked cardboard boxes, and paint cans. Yep, he should've kept in better touch. Joanna's parents had been dead for about four years now, killed in a car wreck when she was only twenty-two. Her Aunt Marcella, if he remembered correctly, was elderly and crippled with arthritis. Jo's only sibling, the younger sister she'd mentioned earlier, was attending college somewhere on the East Coast.

Quickly shoving his thoughts to the back of his mind, he sat down again alongside of Joanna. He struggled to ignore the way the sight of her affected him. His heart hammered. He had to turn away. She was more beautiful that he'd remembered.

***

"Then I'm forgiven?" she asked, smiling. "You won't hold it against me for not letting you know?"

He looked back at her. "Of course not."

Hesitating, running her forefinger over the smooth rim of her coffee mug, she steadied her gaze on him. She took in his high forehead, prominent brow line, and deeply set mocha-colored eyes. His ebony hair was still damp with rain.

"Austin?"

"Hmm?" His gaze held hers.

"Why are you here? Is . . . is everything okay? It's not Mom or Dad. Is it?"

"Oh no!" The reflection from the fire illuminated the planes and angles of his face. "I'm sorry. I didn't intend to alarm you. The folks are fine and their work in Africa is going well."

"Good." She breathed a sigh of relief. Silky, her marmalade-colored calico cat, padded toward her from across the room. She'd been more Kyle's cat than Joanna's, actually. Silky had favored him, jumping on his lap whenever the opportunity arose. Joanna set down her coffee mug on a nearby table and stroked the feline's fur. "So where exactly are you headed?" she finally ventured. "What are your plans?"

"I'm on my way up the coast to check out the fishing in British Columbia. The Queen Charlotte Islands, to be exact. I just thought I'd drop by to say hello."

"Some vacation." Her voice was contrite. "The minute you arrived here, I put you to work." She paused, then added, "But how did you find out that I'd moved?"

"Your neighbor back in Redmond told me, the one across the street. I drove there first, hoping I'd catch you on your day off."

"You must mean Mrs. Ramcourt. The neighbor with the big pine tree in her front yard."

The artery in his neck pulsed. "Yeah, that's the one. Luckily, she remembered meeting me the day of Kyle's services."

Joanna shivered as that familiar gray cloud closed in once again. "Yes . . . the funeral," she murmured. "In some ways it seems like a century ago instead of a little less than a year." Unbidden, the bittersweet picture emerged . . . the tearful eulogies, the entourage of fellow fire fighters who had gather from near and far, the long line of fire trucks that led the funeral procession, Kyle's favorite engine first, carrying his casket.

With a quick shake of her head, Joanna tore her gaze away from Austin and stared back at the fire as if hoping that somehow its warmth would take away the cold, hard pain deep inside of her.

"I barely remember the details of that day," he replied with a catch in his voice. "I guess I was in shock like most everyone else."

"So . . . " She exhaled slowly, steadying herself. "So here we are again. You, footloose-and-fancy-free, passing through town. Me, trying to live in the midst of utter chaos." She waved her hand about the room.

"And your getting caught earlier in a rain squall wasn't total madness," he said. "You were tired of painting and decided to go for a run."

"Yes. How did you guess?"

His somber expression melted into a smile, showing fine laugh lines at the sides of his eyes. "I can see it in your hair. Oyster-shell white, or something like that. Right?"

Self-consciously she combed her hand through her long, wind-tousled strands. She couldn't help but smile too. "Right, but painting's only the beginning. Just look at this place, Austin. Look at all the work it needs: new roof, new carpets, new plumbing."

"Then why did you buy it?" he asked with typical male logic. He settled his back against the couch again, linking his hands behind his head while he waited for her answer.

"This was the only way I could afford to buy beachfront property, to find a fixer-upper that needed plenty of TLC. But when I finally get the work done and can rent out the other side, it should prove a good investment. I need every penny, it seems. Though Stacey was granted a student loan this year, I try to help her out as much as I can."

"Ah, I always figured you had a good head on your shoulders," Austin said. He nodded his approval. "Think you can make all this work?"

"I hope so. As you probably remember, I'm the only family Stacey has, and I feel responsible for her." Her eyes took on a faraway look as she continued, "When we lost our folks in the car accident, Stacey was only a junior in high school, and I had just graduated from Oregon State. For the following year and a half, we shared an apartment together in Redmond, till Stacey left to attend the university and Kyle and I got married . . ." She broke off, chewing on her lower lip.

Their gazes caught and held. Expressive brown eyes so painfully like Kyle's, she thought, with new awareness. Why? Why *now*? She'd just made a clean sweep of her life in an admittedly rash attempt to blot out everything that reminded her of her husband.

But now his older brother was only inches away, threatening to thwart her carefully laid plans. Except for the fact that Austin was nearly three years older, he and Kyle could have passed as identical twins.

He turned to her, regarding her for a second, then sent her a lazy grin. "Sure you're leveling with me, Jo? Sure there wasn't some good-looking lifeguard who talked you into moving here?"

"No way. My only contact here was Aunt Marcella. She was the one who spotted the employment ad for the aquarium and tipped me off." Joanna leveled him an unwavering look. "And as far as men go, the last thing I'm in interested in is romance."

"But why?" A shadow crossed his face.

"Because I'm still in love with Kyle." She felt her throat closing over, the tears springing to her eyes. "I'll always be in love with him." She hesitated, tempted to tell how she'd struggled with the pain, how everywhere she'd turned, there was always something to call forth the memories. But no, Austin had only stopped to say hello, and things were going to get better. He didn't need to know.

***

He averted his gaze. She was tearing him up inside. Any woman with Jo's good looks, corn silk blond hair falling past her shoulders, sparkling blue eyes and porcelain fair skin, shouldn't be sitting around in sackcloth and ashes. Even Kyle—*especially* Kyle—wouldn't have wanted that.

He stared into the dancing flames, remembering too. Kyle. His kid brother, the rebel who insisted on becoming a firefighter, despite their parents' insistence that he follow the family tradition. For three generations now, all the men, their mother too, had been employed in some branch of medicine. But it was he himself who'd encouraged Kyle to follow his dreams, wasn't it? He couldn't deny it. All the more reason he must stick to his word. . . .

***

"Enough about me," she said with forced airiness. "How's your life going in San Francisco? You still enjoying your practice at the zoo?"

"If you can call cocktail parties, research grants, and fund-raising practicing veterinary medicine," he replied. "Though I'm only thirty-one *young* in comparison to the other vets there, lately I've been getting stuck with nearly all of it."

"And that's why you decided you needed to get away?" She really hadn't needed to ask. The stress was obvious, having left its mark on his too handsome face.

"Yep, I was going nuts. The bureaucratic hassles were getting to me." He stared at some indiscernible spot on the opposite wall, mulling over what he needed to do. Truth was, he'd only planned a quick visit with Jo before hitting the road again. He'd figured she'd be getting on with her life without the added pressures of moving, a new job, and major house repairs to boot. But it was obvious now he'd figured wrong. There was no way he could turn his back and leave.

"I'll make you a deal," he said at last. "I'm not too bad with a hammer and nails, you know. I even do plumbing." His gaze flicked over her.

"And?" she prompted. She could see his jaw tense.

"I have several weeks. I'll postpone my fishing trip . . . for just a while. I'll stick around and help you get the duplex back in shape. I could live in the other side in exchange for my labor."

She felt as if someone was squeezing the air out of her lungs. She groped for the first excuse she could muster, but even as she spoke it, she knew it sounded inadequate. "I . . . I don't know, Austin. I mean, what would you do? There's no furniture in the other unit, and I've none to spare. I sold everything I didn't need before the move."

"That's the least of my worries." He settled his elbows on his thighs. "I'm a bachelor, don't forget. And I like it that way. Bottom line is, I prefer living without frills."

"But you're supposed to be on vacation. Why would you want to spend it working?"

"This *will* be a vacation. We'll call it a camping trip, if that makes you happy. I've got a foam pad and bedroll in the back of my Jeep that I keep there for emergencies. I'll throw them down on the floor. And if the other side of the duplex has a room with a view . . . well, what more could I ask for?"

"Thanks, but I'll manage," she insisted. "Kyle and I spent nearly every weekend together remodeling the other house. I learned a lot from him. And what I can't manage alone, I'll contract out."

"You need help," he insisted, ignoring her refusal. "I've got the time and the know-how. Seems to me the rest should be obvious."

She toyed with the hem of her T-shirt. It was tempting. Her job at the Southport Aquarium would leave little free time, and she would indeed need to look for extra help. Besides, this way they'd both be saving money. Since Austin hadn't packed along any camping gear, other than the bedroll he'd mentioned, he probably had planned to stay in motels.

"So it's settled," he said, after she'd hesitated a second too long. He flashed her a disarming smile. "Starting tomorrow morning, eight sharp, consider me your hired hand."

Chapter Two

"He didn't make it," Joanna said to Austin the next evening as she put down her cell phone.

"What?"

"The sea lion died about an hour ago," she clarified. After her first day on the job and a quick trip to the grocery store afterwards, she'd barely stepped in the door before the call from Ted Ashelman had come through.

Austin frowned, setting his paintbrush on the top of the stepladder where he'd been working in the adjoining laundry room. "Too bad," he said, moving toward her, then placing a gentle hand on her shoulder. "Guess we found him a little too late."

She sighed heavily. Despair weighted her voice. "Yes, I'm afraid so. When I phoned Dr. Ashelman first thing this morning from the aquarium, he said the poor animal had taken a turn for the worse and the prognosis wasn't good."

"So you were prepared for bad news."

She shrugged out of her lightweight denim jacket and hung it on the hook behind the kitchen door. "Sort of. But I guess I wasn't willing to throw in the towel till I knew for sure." She sighed again as she twisted a strand of hair around her index finger. "Something's got to be done, Austin. That sea lion didn't have to suffer and die. It's inexcusable for any of our wildlife to suffer like that."

He held her gaze, facing her squarely. "Things are being done. When I drove into town today to pick up more paint, I noticed a poster at Harborman's Lumber about a beach cleanup. It's in a couple of weeks, I think."

"Yes, I know. Trudy Conner, my boss at the aquarium, is the one who put the poster up. Some time ago, she volunteered to be the zone captain for this part of the coast, but she had to resign because of unexpected family obligations. I told her I'd be more than happy to take her place." She reached into the first of two brown paper bags filled with fresh fruit, vegetables, pasta, and assorted cheeses, the staples of her typical vegetarian diet. Silently she opened the refrigerator door and placed a brick of Colby cheese on the top shelf, while he hunched down to stash a five-pound bag of potatoes into a low cupboard.

"Gosh, Jo," he said after a long moment's pause. "This was only your first day on the job. Sure you want to take on all this extra work too?"

"No problem. I like to challenge myself."

"So what'll you have to do?"

"For starters, I'll have to contact the garbage haulers to coordinate the collection sites. Then I must talk with the beach captains in my zone and make sure they understand about setting up the registration sites, checking in volunteers, tallying the collection data cards—that sort of thing." She drew in a deep breath. "Last but not least is the publicity, probably the most significant part of all."

"Meaning, undoubtedly, you'll have to get out the word to the television and radio stations, plus the local and state newspapers."

"Yes, but thank goodness, I'm not working alone." The refrigerator door gave a muffled thud as she shut it. "I'm only one of many who've volunteered on local, state and national levels. Only problem is, it seems many people are still in the dark about the importance of it all. There's never enough volunteers and the problem is especially critical in Southport."

"Why?"

"Because of the town's recent population explosion and popularity with tourists. Our marine wildlife is dying. And if something isn't done, our beaches here will be buried beneath mountains of trash." She pointed to a stack of flyers on the counter. "I've got to start getting these out as soon as possible."

"Let me help you."

Not answering, she wrenched her eyes away from his, struggling to ignore how his nearness disturbed her. It was uncanny . . . and scary. Every time she looked at him, she could only see Kyle.

***

He noticed the sudden shadow darken her face. He saw that desperate, panicked look in her eyes. Was she feeling overwhelmed with the task she'd taken on? Or was she perhaps still thinking about the dead sea lion?

"What is it, Jo? Is something wrong?"

"Has . . . has anyone ever told you how much you look like Kyle?" she finally asked in barely a whisper.

"Yes, all the time." Her reaction caught him totally by surprise. He flinched, his voice ragged. "I'm sorry, Jo. I never considered that. Never for a minute. Maybe I shouldn't have come."

***

She turned to him again and said haltingly, "You needn't apologize, Austin. *I'm* the one who should be sorry. It was selfish of me. Lately, it seems I'm so into myself, preoccupied with my feelings. *But I can't help it*, a small voice inside of her cried. *Especially when you show up like this practically out of the blue. And here we are already, putting away groceries together like Kyle and I used to do.*

He brushed her cheek with the inside of his thumb. His touch was gentle, his skin smooth, clearly the hand of a man who spent more time at fundraisers than engaging in physical labor, she thought. Was his insistence he stay to tackle the necessary repairs really appropriate?

"You're not selfish," he said. "Feelings are feelings and not to be judged."

"Yes, but I'm not the only who's hurting. You lost Kyle too. And what about your parents?"

With furrowed brow, he nodded towards the breakfast nook, a U-shaped green upholstered booth that wrapped around a square oak table. "Sit down. We need to talk."

"About what?"

"About what *really* matters. It's high time we got past the small talk."

Hesitating, she did as he said.

He slipped in across from her, his expression intent as he folded his long legs under the table. "So it sounds as if life has been pretty unbearable these past months . . ."

She poked at a crumb. "Uh-huh. Worse than unbearable. It's been a nightmare, really." She lifted her gaze to his and spied the flecks of gold in his warm brown eyes. The slanting rays of the early evening sun shimmered through the window behind him.

"Why didn't you tell me?" he asked in a low voice. "I'll be the first to admit, I didn't call often enough. But believe me, I would've checked in more if I'd only known."

"I . . . I . . . thought I was strong. I thought I could handle my grief alone." She averted her gaze. "Some people might accuse me of running away, moving to Southport like this, but . . . I had no choice."

He shook his head decisively. "I believe in constructive running away as long as you aren't trying to escape from reality. After all, that's the route my folks took too. They completely uprooted themselves to devote their lives to public service. For them, that has been a powerful healing."

"I'm afraid my escape wasn't nearly so noble," she answered softly, half-apologetically. "It was the memories, Austin, not only my desire to come back to the coast, or because I have an aunt living here. The memories were making me crazy."

He hesitated, rubbing his chin. "I understand. Mom and Dad have their memories, too, twenty-seven years' worth. The house in Seattle where they raised us, Kyle's model car collection, his rubber tire swing still hanging from the giant maple in our backyard . . ." His voice trailed off. "And not a day passes that I don't think of my brother also."

"Oh, Austin . . ." She back-handed the tears coursing down her cheek. Tears of grief. Tears of release. For these past empty months, she'd felt as if no one who'd ever walked the earth could understand her emptiness.

Now her feelings gushed forth like released water from a fractured dyke. "Kyle and I . . . we were so in love. It just wasn't fair . . . that he should die. He was much too young, too good, and full of life. We had too many dreams. Kids. A nice home. Building our careers together. And afterwards . . . after that horrible night, everywhere I turned, there was something to remind me of him. I thought, in time, the feeling would go away. But it didn't. It only tormented me more." She choked back another sob, yet it nevertheless escaped from her lips. "Sometimes at night, sometimes when I couldn't sleep, which was most always, I'd get dressed and drive over to the house where the fire broke out. I'd park on the far side of the street, not wanting to get too close, just sitting there looking at that dreadful, charred monster, wondering what Kyle's last thoughts might've been, wondering whether he suffered."

Austin let out a low groan as he lunged to his feet and captured her hand, pulling her up to him. "Poor Jo . . . how awful. How incredibly awful."

In an instant, his arms encompassed her, and she felt herself melting against his broad chest. The silence stretched between them as they rocked gently, consolingly, sharing their mutual loss. His embrace brought reassurance . . . and a sense of wonder. This man. So big. So strong, just like Kyle.

Austin's voice rumbled against her ear as he continued to hold her. "There's something you should know, Jo. Something that perhaps Kyle never mentioned." Then he pulled back allowing a full arm's length between them.

"What?" she asked.

Hands clasped tightly behind his back, he started to pace, his eyes downcast. "It may be true that Kyle and I look a lot alike," he began tersely, "but that's really where our resemblance ends. He was the rebel, I was the compliant one." She could hear the escalating tension edging his voice, see his frown deepen. "Years ago, when Kyle was a senior in high school and I was living at home and commuting to the university," he continued, "Kyle told Mom and Dad he wasn't going into medicine like everyone else in the family had. At first our parents were livid, then eventually their anger mellowed to bitter disappointment."

"Yes," she said, biting her lip. "Even if Kyle hadn't told me that, I would've sensed it anyway. The weekends your folks visited us, I caught snatches of conversation between Kyle and your father. Though it was obvious all was forgiven, they sometimes still hashed it out."

"At least Kyle didn't leave behind any unresolved issues between them," he said as he stopped to angle her a look.

"Yes, thank goodness." She paused, then encouraged, "But getting back to your story about Kyle's senior year . . ."

He started pacing again. "Yes. That was a difficult time. And I guess I didn't help matters either."

"What do you mean?"

"Secretly, I admired my little brother's gutsiness, though at first I was careful not to let our folks know. Even if I had wanted to be something other than a veterinarian, I knew that I, the dutiful elder son, would never have had the courage to strike out on my own like Kyle. Call it the prodigal son story—whatever, that's how it happened."

"But did Kyle rebel only to be different, or did he truly want to be a firefighter?" she asked. From every indication she'd gleaned, Kyle's dedication to the department had always been totally sincere.

Austin leaned against the opposite wood-paneled wall and pinned her with his gaze. "Kyle wanted it. Pure and simple. Even when he was a little kid, his favorite toy trucks were fire engines. When he moved on to high school, then had to choose a senior project before graduation, he applied for volunteer training at the local substation not far from our home."

"So it shouldn't have come as any big surprise to your parents when Kyle made his final announcement," she pointed out.

"No, it shouldn't have, but it did. I guess they were holding out hope till the very last minute." He picked up a color photograph of his brother from the corner bookshelf and turned it over. His voice grew thick with emotion. "When things got really heated, I finally broke my silence and openly sided with Kyle. I . . . I was the one who encouraged him to stick to his dreams, Jo. I even helped him send away for information, traveled with him to various community colleges to help him determine which one offered the best fire science program." He set the picture back down, his jaw rigid. "If I hadn't done that, maybe Kyle would be alive today."

"Oh, no, Austin!" She couldn't hold back the alarm from her voice. "You mustn't beat yourself up that way!"

A muscle in his neck twitched. "And if that's not bad enough," he went on as through not having heard her, "now I come along and remind you of Kyle. Maybe I *should* leave, Jo. Maybe my being here is sabotaging your very reason for relocating."

"No. Please stay." Her words sounded distant, as if spoken by someone else. Perhaps it was her ambivalence that had muted that plea, she couldn't be sure. While one part of her urged to send him immediately on his way, the other part yearned for his continued presence. "I'll get through it, honest I will. I think . . . I think I'm starting to already."

"Oh?"

She nodded. "Yesterday when we visited Anchorhold, and I could see for myself the good work going on there, I felt a little more alive. I began to care about the things that have always been important to me—the marine wildlife and birds, preserving our planet."

She sat back down at the breakfast nook again and added with quiet conviction, "I'm ready now to get back in touch with that part of my life. It may not be everything, but at least it's a start."

"And you already started even before that," he pointed out, sliding in again across from her. "Accepting your new job at the aquarium, to my way of thinking, was your first big step.'

***

He studied her silently. He hoped she was right. He hoped against all hope she was beginning to heal. And if that were true, maybe his job wouldn't be so tough after all. Or tougher, another inner voice argued.

The sudden realization was unnerving. Maybe he'd be sorry he'd ever gotten into this mess. He'd offered to help with the duplex, not continuously take time out to assist the injured seabirds and other animals she would undoubtedly endear herself to. Bottom line was, he might never get up to that fishing resort in Canada. The sound of her talking snatched him from his thoughts.

"I wonder how many people realize that birds, fish, and mammals sometimes mistake plastic throwaways for food?" she was going on. "Some seabirds, gulls, puffins, and murres even try to feed it to their offspring." Though he'd missed the earlier part of what she'd been saying, he could tell her words had been fueled with missionary zeal. Waving a hand as she talked, her cheeks were flushed and glistening.

He regarded her for a moment longer, his former wariness soon forgotten. He'd never known anyone quite like Joanna Sullivan. She was invigorating. Refreshing. Like the mountain spring waters she could most likely also fight to preserve, if ever called upon to. Did she have any idea how pretty she was when she got all fired up like that? Even prettier than usual, if that were possible.

"Well?" she stopped short, waiting for his confirmation. "Don't you agree, Austin?"

"Ah . . .of course. Every word." He flashed her a smile, leaned back against the booth and folded his arms across his chest, but the look on his face suggested he might only be humoring her.

She pulled back her shoulders. "So you think I'm nothing more than a yammering sentimentalist, is that it?"

"No one said any such thing."

"Then why were you so quiet?"

"I've never known anyone like you, Jo," he answered at last. Though his smile reached his dark eyes with a teasing awareness, his voice had turned genuine. "I mean, everyone I know seems to be living in the fast lane these days. Too busy to care about what happens to our wildlife."

She lifted one shoulder. "You don't have to flatter me. I don't expect you to understand completely. Like Ted Ashelman said, the concept of wildlife rehab is still relatively new."

"Yes. And I have to admit, I was one of those who were schooled in traditional veterinary medicine." He toyed with the saltshaker on the table, peering down at the small white granules sticking to the top. Then he lifted his eyes to meet hers. "But don't give up on me entirely. I'm not so old and set in my ways that I can't learn from people like you." He winked, sending her a broad smile.

***

Without answering, she stood up and crossed the small room. As she paused to stare out the white-paned window that looked onto the beach, her throat went dry, her hands grew clammy. Why was she reacting this way? she asked herself. He'd only winked, for heaven's sales. And his brotherly hug a few minutes earlier had been merely to console her.

"Listen," he said, getting to his feet too. "How long has been since you've had a night on the town?"

"A while."

"Since before Kyle died?"

"Yes." She felt him standing close beside her, but kept her gaze focused straight ahead. The faint hint of his musky after-shave wafted about her.

"Then I think you're long overdue."

"If you're talking a night on the town in Southport," she said, "then you're going to be in for a big disappointment." In spite of herself, she turned to him and smiled. "All the shop owners here roll up their sidewalks at six sharp."

"Ah, but not tonight. The rest of the week either."

"What are you talking about?"

"The annual kite festival. The paper said it started this morning and runs all week long. There's lots of evening activities music, displays, and good food."

"Oh, that's right! How could I have forgotten? The aquarium was packed today because of all the extra tourists in town." Her eyes drifted to the *Seascroll*, a weekly local newspaper that had arrived that morning and was lying on the breakfast nook table. An article about the celebrated event was plastered across the front page, but she'd been in such a hurry to get out the door, she'd barely skimmed it.

"So, what do you say?" he asked again, his voice unmistakably eager.

"I . . . I don't know. I really need to check on Aunt Marcella tonight. She has a neighbor who runs errands for her, but I help too."

"Where does she live?"

"About three miles south of here."

"Then we can check on her together before we go into town. Tonight might even be a good time to get out the flyers about the beach cleanup. As I mentioned earlier, I'd like to help."

She hesitated again. While she was overjoyed that he wanted to assist her, she also realized this could be one added complication to their already strained situation. The sound of his voice pulled her back.

"It goes without saying, two can cover more territory than one." He gestured enthusiastically as he spoke. "And besides, I'd like to meet Aunt Marcella. Somehow I missed doing that the day you and Kyle got married."

"That's because she wasn't there. Auntie had a flare-up of arthritis and couldn't leave her house."

"Then that settles it. What are we waiting for?" He held out her denim jacket, waiting for her to slip inside. "Shall we take your car or my Jeep?"

"My Subaru will be fine." She wriggled into the jacket, refusing to admit to herself how his magnetic persuasiveness had just destroyed her resolve.

***

As evening shadows lengthened, Southport was a riot of color, sights, and sounds. The afternoon kite-flying contest long since over, many of the festival-goers had turned back from the beach, leaving behind those who'd lingered to build sand castles, picnic, and watch an orange-mauve sunset.

Joanna and Austin had spent the first hour visiting Aunt Marcella, who'd basked in their company, all the while studying Austin speculatively through cataract-clouded eyes. After they'd said good-night and driven back to the duplex, they decided to walk the rest of the way into town. The skies remained clear, and already the side streets were gridlocked with traffic.

"One more small way to fight pollution," Joanna pointed out, half-serious, half-whimsical. "Besides, it's such a beautiful evening, it'd be a shame not to take full advantage of it."

"Agreed," he said with a widening smile. "And after spending most of the afternoon stuck on a ladder painting, I certainly could use a good walk."

They meandered down the two-mile boardwalk that bordered the beach, then stopped to dine on creamy clam chowder and crusty grilled cheese bread at a popular seafood restaurant in the center of town.

While they sat beneath a canopied table on a wraparound deck overlooking the ocean, she told him about the beach walk she would be leading the following morning and the large numbers of people who'd already signed up.

He told her about his work at the duplex, painting, fixing three rotted windowpanes, and ordering supplies.

Though their conversation flowed, businesslike and safe again, they each were aware of the ever-constant current of tension, like an invisible shield between them. She still wrestled with her decision to let him stay. He still battled with his sense of obligation.

Soon they left the restaurant and approached Main Street, now temporarily blocked off to traffic. Everywhere, people roamed. Young couples strolled arm-in-arm, teenagers munched on pink cotton candy, parents pushed baby strollers, and retired folks sported neon-colored warm-up suits and trendy walking shoes. Some paused beneath streetlights to admire sidewalk chart art in dusty pastels, while others listened to the foot-stomping sounds from the old-time fiddlers in the town square. Store windows displayed "Open" signs and shoppers, in search of the perfect souvenir, filtered in and out.

From concession stands in a nearby lot, the tantalizing smells of hamburgers, hot dogs, and tacos carried on the tangy salt air breeze. At sunset, a gauzy full moon peeped above the east horizon.

"If we hadn't just eaten, I could get hungry all over again," Joanna said with a chuckle as they paused outside a candy store that featured saltwater taffy. "All these wonderful aromas are driving me crazy!" She blinked, amazed what she'd just said. Ever since Kyle had died, she'd lost all interest in food. Truth was, she had nearly wasted away from a size ten to a size six.

"Yeah, nothing better than the smell of good food in the great outdoors," he agreed, digging into the deep pockets of his beige windbreaker. Quickly, he produced the packet of flyers, held in place by a thick rubber band. "All right, you're the boss. Where should we start?"

"I'll take the east side of the street, you take the west."

"Fair enough. Let's meet back here when we're done. I wouldn't expect to be much later than an hour or so. Looks as if the business district on Main Street doesn't take up much more than six blocks." He winked. "And if I get back here before you do, I'll buy you some taffy."

She smiled back at him, feeling her face grow warm. Maybe her first intention tonight had been to mix business with pleasure, but already the scales were tipping off balance. Spending time with Austin was definitely all pleasure, no matter how you sliced it.

When they'd finished, flyers were plastered in storefront windows and stacked on nearly every checkout counter. Already folks could be seen wandering about with the eye-catching announcement clutched in their hands.

"Good news!" Joanna said to Austin as they fell in step with the rest of the crowd, moving closer to the sounds of the fiddlers. "While you were at the surplus shop, I managed to talk to Joe Oretega, the district Boy Scout coordinator, into getting several troops involved. The beach cleanup and the scout outing at Camp Meriweather fall on the same weekend, so the timing was perfect! The camp's only two miles down the highway, you know."

"Good news indeed," Austin said. "Cooperation like that should pack a wallop."

"Yes, and if I'm figuring right, that'll add up to a couple hundred extra volunteers to help clean the beaches." They passed storefront windows decked out in an array of logo T-shirts, beach hats, and sporting equipment. Austin cupped his palm over the small of her back.

"Austin?" she asked, turning to him. His touch felt warm and very masculine.

"Yes, Jo?"

"You . . . you haven't really said. Do you plan to help on the day of the beach cleanup?"

"Maybe. That depends how much work I can get done at the duplex in the next two weeks."

"Oh." She kept her voice even, determining not to let her disappointment show. For some reason, she wasn't sure why, it would be a comfort to know, for the short time at least, that there'd be a man close by to talk to. The long, lonely evenings had indeed left their mark.

They rounded the next corner past a hanging flower basket that cascaded with scarlet and pink petunias. The upbeat sounds of "Fiddler's Dream" grew louder. Three men, two thirtyish and clean-shaven, the third who wore a gray busy beard and a red flannel shirt stood atop a red, white, and blue canopied platform with violins tucked under their chins. Their polished instruments glinted beneath the overhead spot lights. Their bows seesawed in perfect three-quarter time.

Drawn, Joanna and Austin took their places at the back of the crowd. Off to the side, a handful of grade-school-aged children were skipping in a wide circle in time to the melody. A dog yapped. In the distance, the shrill whine of an ambulance siren momentarily drowned out the cacophony of music, shouts, and laughter.

The gala ambiance was captivating, infectious. Once again, Joanna's heart felt buoyant and carefree. The ocean breeze rising up from the beach rippled through her long blond hair, tousling the strands that fell loosely at the sides of her face. The night was balmy. Overhead, a shooting start streaked across the heavens. The full moon rode higher.

As the music flowed on, she cast a quick look at Austin, who was obviously enjoying himself too. An easy smile lifted his lips while he tapped his foot rhythmically. Beneath his open jacket, he was wearing a dusty blue polo shirt and faded jeans that accentuated his muscled legs and lean hips. The hint of a five o'clock shadow showed about the lower half of his face, making him appear even more ruggedly handsome.

They remained, listening to one tune after the next till at last the fiddlers loosened the hair on their bows and positioned their instruments back into felt-lined cases. But as Joann and Austin started their leisurely trek back home, drinking in the wonder of the autumn night, her mind was plagued with disturbing new questions.

How had this happened? What was she doing here with her husband's brother?

Chapter Three

Back at the duplex, Joanna and Austin stood beneath the porch light. The leaves of the Japanese maple that edged the walkway were motionless now, the breeze stilled. On the lawn, shimmers of dew caught the moonlight like thousands of minute rainbows. Crickets chirped.

"Well, here we are," he said, willing nonchalance into his voice. "Hope you had a good time."

"I had a wonderful time. Thanks for suggesting it and thanks, too, for helping."

"My pleasure."

They talked about when the workers would come to lay the new carpet and whether she would need to buy more paint.

"I'm eager to start redecorating the guest bedroom as soon as possible," she said with a smile. "Don't you think a soft sea foam green would go well in there?"

Nodding, he smiled back, then stared down into her wide, blue eyes. "Good choice."

"I appreciate everything you're doing, Austin," she continued. "I realize now I set myself up for more than I could handle alone."

"I'm just glad I managed to track you down. If I hadn't taken this vacation, I would've still thought you were living back in Redmond." He caught her hand in his and gave it a quick squeeze.

"Like I said before, I never meant to isolate myself. Still, it was thoughtless of me."

"No. Not thoughtless. Not given the circumstances." He knew he should let go of her hand, but somehow couldn't. "You . . . you'd better get in now," he urged hoarsely. "You'll want to be rested. Tomorrow morning will come early." He hesitated, then asked. "You going to run on the beach again?"

"Six o'clock. Same time as always."

Once corner of his mouth quirked up in a smile. "It was almost four-thirty in the afternoon when I found you yesterday, nearly drenched with rain and totally beside yourself."

"Yes, but that was my second run of the day," she pointed out. She swallowed hard as she pushed aside a picture of the injured sea lion, then wondered why he'd asked about her running. He'd never indicated he was a runner too. Probably just curious, or filling their admittedly awkward parting with whatever first came to his mind.

He took one step back and jammed his hands into his hip pockets. "Good night, Jo. See you tomorrow."

"'Night, Austin." She'd planned to inform him she'd leave out some cash in an envelope on the kitchen counter in case he might need to buy new supplies. But somehow that had all paled now. Paled in the power of his piercing gaze, the backwash of his brief touch.

"Sleep well," she added, her throat suddenly dry. She turned slowly to insert her key in the lock. Two moths fluttered together beneath the porch light, then zigzagged away.

"I will. You too."

***

Austin paced. He'd been pacing for close to an hour. Man, how he detested this lousy habit. He'd practically worn a threadbare patch back in his condo, mulling over his problems at the zoo. Would the grant moneys come through on time? Would this city official or that philanthropist approve his request for increased funding? And now here he was again. Pacing. Good thing *this* carpet was already shot. If he hadn't sworn off cigarettes a few years back, he'd probably be sending up smoke signals right now too.

"Look, little bro," he ground out. "I'm doing what you asked, okay? I always knew you and Jo shared something special, something I could never quite understand, even if I was the marrying type. But it's tough being here with her. Tougher than I'm sure either you or I expected." He halted in his tracks, shrugged, and spread his hands wide.

"Well, anyway, I don't mean to sound as if I'm complaining, because I'm not really. You know I never break a promise, and I don't intend to change now. You can count on me. Can you believe it, Kyle? She hasn't even enjoyed a night out since . . . since, well, you know what."

He squared his jaw and swallowed hard before continuing. "You wouldn't want that. I know you too well, little bro. You were always too concerned about the other guy more than Kyle Sullivan. That's what got you into that mess in the first place, didn't it? Rushing into that burning house to save those two little kids." His voice broke, but he nevertheless ranted on. "So anyway, about tonight . . . I . . . I confess I had to bait Jo just a little. Oh, it's not that I don't share her interest in the beach cleanup. I do. But I couldn't help thinking if I offered to help get the brochures out, I could help her out too. And right now, I'm afraid that's what she needs the most."

His thoughts strayed back to how her eyes had looked that night. Eyes so trusting. *Too* trusting. No wonder his brother had fallen so hard for her. It was a surprise, really, some other guy hadn't fallen too these past months. Yet it was obvious no one would've stood a prayer—not with the thick concrete walls Jo had built around herself.

***

Joanna slept fitfully. A hazy stream of half-conscious thoughts spun like a Ferris wheel through her dreamless sleep: thoughts about tomorrow's beach walk, worries about handling the barrage of questions that would undoubtedly accompany it, plans to call the print shop to order another couple hundred brochures.

But intruding upon her restless thoughts were images of Austin and herself strolling in the misty moonlight on their way back from town. Each time that picture swam up in her mind, she'd awakened with a start, perplexed and guilt-ridden. Yes, it was all so confusing, and somehow not right. Not right for Austin, herself, nor Kyle's memory. Even the sound of Silky's throaty purr as she lay curled on the end of the bed failed to soothe Joanna as it usually did.

When daylight finally poked its brightening gray fingers across the sky, she forced herself out of bed to don running shorts and a T-shirt. All she needed was an extra long run to clear her head, she told herself with a swift mental shake. A good workout *should* help.

Soon she wended her way down the trail that led to the beach. Picking her way over driftwood and rocks, she approached the ribbon of compact sand that bordered the water's edge.

Early morning on the beach, before the usual crowds filtered in, marked her favorite time. Today the skies were crystal clear, splashed with rose-tinted peach to the east. Above the ridge of dark evergreens, the sun emerged, ushering in the promise of another pristine autumn day.

She paused, then stretched out her muscles in a runner's lunge and inhaled deeply. Yes, she'd run that extra mile or two, maybe more. Test her limits. Surely that's all it would take to get her thoughts back in line.

Facing south, she began sprinting. The morning breeze lifted her hair. The air rushed by her. Running faster, she felt the coolness expanding her lungs, the hypnotic rhythm of her footfall.

Kyle, she thought. *Why did you have to leave me? Why, when we were just beginning our lives together? How could fate have so abruptly cut off our plans?* Sometimes she felt like holding up her fist and shaking it in anger. Crying over and over how it simply wasn't fair. Yes, this past year she must've relived that scene in her mind a thousand times.

And now there was Austin. When would she *ever* find peace? she wondered as she sidestepped a log that had washed in on the tide. Last night their leisurely walk home had nearly been her undoing.

She ran the first mile, began the next. She felt the perspiration trickle down onto her sweatband. As she pressed on, her tormented thoughts turned to her younger sister.

The past week Stacey had called several times. Apparently she'd fallen in love with an upperclassman, a really cool new man on campus, she'd said, who was in pre-law. But Stacey was also in a quandary. Was it possible to love two guys at once? she'd asked Joanna over and over. No matter how hard she tried, she couldn't forget the guy she'd met the preceding summer, the one who lived an hour's drive from campus and drove there nearly every weekend to be with her.

Some wise big sister I am, Joanna told herself as she skirted past a solitary beachcomber, then a collie that was darting across the sand, barking. How could she pass on any solid advice when, in all honesty, she no longer understood the workings of her own heart?

Oh, Austin. Why did I agree to let you stay?

She kept on, pushing herself to the max. Yet by the time she'd come to the end of the beach and turned to go back, it was apparent there was no relief in sight.

Her demons still plagued her.

***

"Come in, Joanna." Trudy Conner, willowy tall with soft ringlets of blond hair, motioned Joanna inside her office at the aquarium. "It's high time I say thanks for taking over for me. What with soccer practice, music lessons, and gymnastics, I just couldn't follow through as zone captain for the beach cleanup this year." She angled a look at her desk calendar and added, "My gosh, is it really less than two weeks away?"

"I'm more than happy to help," Joanna answered as she sat down in a chair on the other side of the desk. "Last night when I got out the rest of the flyers in town, the response to the cleanup was encouraging."

"And how are the other preparations coming along?"

"Fine. A little while ago I left messages for the beach captains in this zone to contact me. The data cards and collection bags have just arrived, so I need to make sure everyone gets what they need. I also intend to check out all the beaches to get a better idea where the most debris is."

"Start with the campgrounds," Trudy suggested. "It goes without saying that's one of the high-use areas."

"Yes, and the public beach below my duplex too," Joanna added. She went on to explain about the sea lion and the other marine wildlife at the rehab center. "If everyone visited there only once, I'm sure the need for cleanups would be easily cut in half."

Trudy nodded in agreement as she tapped the end of a pen against the desk. "And I bet most people don't realize that some of the compounds from plastic throwaways will last for hundreds of years, whether part of a landfill or floating on the ocean. In fact, I was just about to call a woman at the Marine Fisheries Service to discuss that. She's putting together a special project to display here sometime next month."

Trudy had been the aquarium business manager for the past six years, and the facility was flourishing. She appeared a true Super Mom, Joanna thought. A woman who could successfully juggle a career and motherhood.

Today, less than an hour after opening, scores of tourists streamed into the modern L-shaped interior with its high slanted ceilings and expansive picture windows. Some stood gawking through thick windows at a Pacific octopus undulating through the murky water while striped bass and copper rockfish flitted in and out of mock pilings. Other visitors examined tidal pool displays where red, purple, and green sea anemones flourished like translucent spiny flowers. On the outer edges of the pools, barnacles clung to rocks and sea lettuce and kelp provided a lush, green carpet.

In a direct line from Trudy's office stood the "handling tank." Children huddled about it, turning over a spiny red-orange starfish as they peered at its cuplike tentacles.

"So what's the final tally on the number of campers who've signed up for the beach walk?" Joanna asked, her thoughts turning to her first major assignment of the day.

"Last check, about—" A sudden exclamation of protest from one of the children sliced through her next words. "Kids!" Trudy said, shaking her head and grinning.

Joanna followed Trudy's gaze through the opened door where two girls and a boy were engaged in obvious disagreement over who should first hold the starfish. A young mother with a toddler in tow attempted to referee.

"Brother and sisters, no doubt," Trudy said with a laugh. "At least judging from the way they're arguing, I assume that's the case."

"Typical growing pains, I guess," Joanna supplied.

"Yes, they remind me so much of my own kids. Enemies one minute. Long-lost friends the next. But believe me, they're the light of my life." She gestured towards a brass-framed photo on the corner of her desk. Three cherubic-faced children smiled back, posed in stair-step fashion.

"Oh, my . . ." Joanna breathed. "All sunny smiles and blond curls, just like yours."

"Yes, but if you think they're beautiful, you should see my husband, Grant. I think the kids get more of their looks from him than me."

The sound of contentment in Trudy's voice made Joanna's heart turn over. Once she'd thought she could have all that too. But now it would never happen.

Trudy glanced down at Joanna's engagement ring topped by a silver wedding band. The diamond flashed, catching a beam of sunlight. "Do you have children, Joanna?"

"Uh. No." Suddenly self-conscious, Joanna twisted the rings back and forth. "More than anything, I wish I did," she added. After a moment's hesitation, Joanna went on to explain about Kyle.

"Oh, I'm so sorry," Trudy murmured. "Such a tragedy. Such a horrible story." She attempted a feeble smile. "I . . . I didn't mean to pry. I noticed your ring and thought maybe—"

"No need to apologize," Joanna broke in, squaring her shoulders and looking away. "No need at all. I'm getting along just fine now." She felt a lump tighten at the base of her throat as that sense of loss threatened to overtake her again.

But deep inside a new awareness gnawed. It's *been almost a year, Joanna. Maybe it's time to take the rings off.*

***

That evening, Joanna found Austin pounding nails into the front porch where he was replacing several rotted boards. "There's more stuff going on in town tonight," he reminded her, putting his hammer inside his toolbox. "Would you like to go back, maybe check out the street dance near the boardwalk?" He flashed her a devilish grin and added, "I might even be able to help you find some good-looking bachelor."

"I already told you. I'm not interested in meeting another man."

"You can't go on like this forever, Jo. You're young. And very attractive. You have your whole life ahead of you."

"I don't intend to," she stammered. "It's just that . . . that the time's not quite right yet. And I have to take care of some other things first . . . and then, it might still be a long, long time." Something deep inside stabbed at her as her gaze dropped momentarily to her wedding rings. "Besides, we're out of flyers," she added in a rush, lifting her eyes again. "So there's really no point in going back into town. The printer said he can't fill my order for more until sometime next week."

"Suit yourself." He shrugged.

Joanna took in Austin's furrowed brow, the disappointed look in his warm brown eyes. *Poor guy,* she thought. *He's probably bored silly. Imagine, someone from an exciting, sophisticated metropolis like San Francisco, wanting to go two nights in a row to a homespun kite festival in a quaint little coastal town.*

"I have an older television in the guest bedroom," she offered. "If you'd like to take it to your side, please do. It's an extra, and I won't need it." She was tempted now to invite him to spend the evening with her watching a movie on Neflix or listening to music, but she didn't. Their romantic evening last night had proved a big mistake.

Besides, she needed plenty of space tonight. Time alone. Yes, tonight was the night. If she didn't take off her wedding rings while she still had the nerve, she might change her mind. "I have a better idea. How about taking in a flick at the cinema down the highway?"

"No thanks. I really should turn in early."

"All right. Then I'll settle on your offer to take the TV. He jerked his head to one side. "I'll go get it right now."

A few minutes later, she held open the front door and watched him leave, carrying the TV across the lawn. "Good-night," she called, struggling to keep her voice even.

"See you tomorrow."

Shutting the door, she bit her lip and heaved a sigh. Yes, tomorrow. Tomorrow would be a brand new day. But right now she had all she could do to deal with the remainder of tonight.

She wandered into her bedroom and switched on the wall lamp near the doorway. Soft light flooded the room. On top of the bureau was her burgundy velvet jewelry box.

Kyle. Her gaze drifted to his photo next to it. His image smiled back at her, the smile that always flashed in her mind whenever she thought about him. She must've had a dozen or more pictures of Kyle situated around the duplex, she thought with a pang. But this one had always been her favorite. Balling her hands into fists, she pulled her eyes away.

Through the bedroom walls, from the other side, she heard the muffled tones of the television. Cheerful sounds. A sitcom, perhaps. Canned laughter.

Slowly she lifted the lid of the jewelry box. In the uppermost compartment, nestled in the plush layer of velvet was the simple gold band she'd given Kyle on their wedding day. Seeing it, her heart seemed to turn inside out. What was she doing, taking off her rings too? she wondered desperately. Was she turning her back on everything that they'd shared? The good times, and sometimes not so good? Their hopes and dreams? Their plans for the future?

"Oh, Kyle," she murmured, tears springing to her eyes. "You do understand, don't you? This . . . this is something I've put off, but now I must do it. The time is right. But please know, I'll cherish your memory always. I'll always love you."

She swallowed hard. It felt as if an ice cube was lodged in the throat. The tears fell, one after the next, tracking salty trails down her cheeks as she twisted the rings over her knuckles and then slipped them completely off.

In the lamp light, the diamond sparkled, flashing prisms of light. She traced her finger over it, then for a moment held it up to her lips. Blinking rapidly, hands trembling, she placed it in the jewelry box next to the gold band, shut the lid, then turned and walked away.

Through the bedroom walls, she could still hear the sounds of canned laughter.

Chapter Four

"Finally," Austin muttered. He lay braced on one elbow, legs sprawled as he studied the pipes beneath the kitchen sink.

"What's going on?" Joanna plunked down a bag of groceries on the counter and grinned at him. Faint wisps of hair poked out from both sides of her French braid, giving her a pleasantly disheveled appearance. It had been blustery, though sunny, at Two Capes State Park and today's beach walk had lasted longer than usual.

"A piece of pipe broke off inside a fitting," he answered. "I got it out just before you walked in. Now all I have to do is replace the pipe itself."

"Anything I can do to help?"

"Yeah. Hand me the wrench and flashlight, please. They're right there in the bottom of my toolbox."

She squatted, sorting through the tools, then handed over what he needed.

"You might also park yourself close by," he said. "This could take a while."

A little more than two weeks had passed since Austin had arrived. By now, helping him had become second nature to her.

She sat down on the floor, cross-legged, and slipped her left hand into the pocket of her denim jacket. How bare and exposed her hand felt, she thought again, for what seemed like the hundredth time. If Austin had noticed that she was no longer wearing her rings, he'd given no indication.

His face lined with concentration, Austin snapped on the flashlight and beamed it onto the pipes and fittings.

"Right now I'm just checking out everything else," Austin explained, slicing through her thoughts. "I want to make sure none of the other pipes are cracked also. As old as this plumbing is, I wouldn't be surprised to discover more than one problem." He paused. "Have a good day?"

"Yes. How about you? Aside from this little plumbing problem, that is."

"Busy. This morning I made another stop at the builder's supply. They said the roofing materials are on the way. About time."

"Oh, that reminds me," she put in. "Trudy said that when we're ready to get to work on the roof, her husband will be happy to give us a hand. He's in real estate now, but he used to be a professional roofer."

"Good. We'll need all the help we can get."

"So how does the plumbing look?" she asked, chewing on a fingernail. Silently she prayed there wouldn't be any more problems. Even with Austin doing the repairs, the cost of materials was mounting quickly.

"Surprisingly, everything else appears A-OK. Now to get back to that broken pipe." He slanted her a look. "Come here. I need you to hold this flashlight."

"All right." She felt her pulse racing as she slid in alongside of him. Suddenly he was only inches away, much too near. As she aimed the light onto the spot where he was working, she stared at the dark hairs on the back of his strong, tanned hands, heard his steady, gentle breathing. The cramped quarters smelled wet and musty from where the pipe had been leaking.

"I intended to stop by at Anchorhold on my way home from work," she told him, struggling to ignore the way he was affecting her. "But road construction waylaid my plans. I was forced to detour onto Grieger's Road, which bypasses the rehab clinic completely."

A few days earlier, Joanna had rescued another injured animal—this time a great horned owl with a broken wing. When she'd found the bird perched inside her storage shed, it had appeared stunned and frightened. Not wanting to burden Austin further, she'd fashioned a sling for the owl from an old stocking cap, given it sugar water with an eyedropper, then driven it to Anchorhold.

"I suppose you wanted to check on your fine-feathered friend," he drawled. He clamped the wrench onto the end of the broken pipe and started twisting.

"The owl?"

"Uh-huh."

"Of course I did."

"Well, I beat you to it." He slanted her a look.

"Oh?" She couldn't hold back the surprise in her voice.

"I stopped in myself on the way back from the builders' supply—before the road crews had moved that far up the highway. I also ended up staying awhile to give Ted a hand. His intern had called in sick that day."

"So how is the owl doing?" she broke in anxiously.

"His wing appears to be healing nicely and he's also eating again."

"What's the matter?" Joanna asked, temporarily distracted. She couldn't help noticing he still hadn't managed to dislodge the pipe.

"Fittings are a little rusty. No sweat, though. I'll have this baby out of here in no time."

For the next few minutes, he worked on in silence, twisting and turning, while Joanna continued to hold the flashlight. Her arm was growing heavy and all she really yearned to do after another busy day was slip out of her work clothes and luxuriate in a hot shower. But being close to Austin like this was rather nice, and who was she to complain? After all, he was postponing his trip to help her, wasn't he? She still couldn't fathom why he had taken on such an immense commitment. Hanging around for a few days was one thing, but forsaking most, if not all, of his vacation? It still didn't add up.

"Don't get what?"

"Here you are, doing all this for me, when what you really need is that fishing trip. Are you sure you don't mind?"

He glanced over at her. "Maybe. Maybe not. But like I already said, the seals and sea lions are eating most of the salmon anyway."

"Yes, but that's not the only reason the salmon are disappearing," she was quick to point out. "Chemicals in the streams and oceans are killing them too. So is human debris." She felt her face grow warm with annoyance. Was it really necessary to bring that prickly topic up one more time?

"You can put the flashlight down now," he said, ignoring her response. "I'm almost done."

She considered momentarily, then asked. "Shouldn't you be using two wrenches instead of one? Kyle always used to."

"Nah. Not for a simple job like this."

Unexpectedly, she felt something furry brushing against her ankles, then edging between their shoulders. "Silky!" she scolded, darting a glance at the calico feline.

Joanna reached out a hand to gently push the cat away, but Silky managed to sashay past them, purring throatily. In seconds, the cat was poking her nose beneath the pipes and connectors.

"Don't you love the sound of a cat purring?" Joanna asked dreamily. "Nothing like it after a long day."

"Right now, no!" The wrench slipped out of his hand and clattered to the floor. Do something, Jo. Get Slinky out of here!"

"Silky," she corrected. She handed him back the wrench.

"Okay, Silky then."

She had every intention of retrieving the cat, but couldn't resist teasing him a little. "What's the matter, Austin? You're the big game vet. Certainly one solitary feline shouldn't throw you off course."

A curious Silky continued to purr and explore, pausing to rub her head affectionately against Austin's shoulder.

"Forget the vet bit," he growled, though the grin on his face betrayed him. "Right now, I'm the plumber. If you expect me to get this pipe fixed, then you'll have to do something about this confounded ca—" he jerked back, almost hitting his head against hers while frigid water spewed forth in all directions. "Whoa!"

The cat bolted out of sight.

Joanna shrieked.

Austin lunged to his feet. "Where's the main shut-off valve?" he shouted.

Joanna, still supine, was laughing so hard the tears streamed down her face. "I . . . I don't know," she managed at last, gripping her stomach as a new wave of belly laughs threatened. She swiped away new tears as she stared up at his large form looming over her. He looked wonderful—in a very drenched sort of way. Dark hair, disheveled and shining. Soaked white T-shirt straining against his chest. She suddenly realized she was drenched too.

"You don't know!" he bellowed.

"I . . . I never got around to checking it out."

"Women!" He shook his head, then raced outside, undoubtedly in search of the water meter, while she scrambled to her feet. Meanwhile, she rummaged wildly through the drawers she'd stocked with kitchen towels, grabbing up several at a time.

She was on her hands and knees, mopping up puddles and still chuckling to herself when he returned, the emergency now under control.

"I don't see what's so damn funny," he muttered.

"I'm sorry about the cat, Austin. I was just about to remove her, but . . . but . . ." She burst into another round of laughter, then got to her feet again, this time a bit shakily. "What happened anyway?"

"I loosened the wrong connection. I unfastened the shut-off valve instead of the broken pipe."

"That's why Kyle always used to use two wrenches," she said. "One to loosen the pipe, the second to keep the shut-off valve from slipping."

His expression hardened. "I'm not Kyle. Stop comparing me to him!"

"Oh!" Joanna felt the blood rush to her head. The room started to spin. "I . . . I didn't mean it that way—"

"Face it." He cut her off with a wave of his hand. "How can you help *not* making comparisons?"

She bit her lip. He was right. She'd fallen into her own trap. First she'd told Austin how much he resembled Kyle, then she'd implied he wasn't measuring up to him. Perhaps she should've encouraged Austin to leave when he'd first suggested it.

"I can see there's something we've got to get straight," he went on tersely. He took one step closer, towering over her. "No matter what happens from here on in, I refuse to live in Kyle's shadow."

Squaring her shoulders, she summoned her composure. "You seem to be overlooking one obvious difference. Kyle and I were man and wife . . . soul mates. We'd pledged to spend our lives together. You're my brother-in-law. You're only here to help. Just for a while."

"Yes . . . just for a while," he echoed. He looked away. His voice dropped. "Kyle was good. No, he was *more* than good. The best. No matter how hard I might try, I could never fill his shoes."

"But that's not true. You were the one who stuck by your parents' wishes. You told me yourself Kyle was a rebel."

He met her gaze again. "Yes, but he was also a hero. A hero who perished saving two little kids' lives. A hero who should've never died in the first place." He inhaled a ragged breath, stifling a sob. His eyes, dark and haunted, mirrored his pain.

Instinctively, she closed the distance between them and flung her arms around his broad chest. "Oh, Austin . . ."

"Jo, Jo, what's the use?" he murmured against her ear, pulling her closer. "What's the use trying to figure it all out."

"Shh!" she whispered, stroking the side of his head. "Don't try."

He heaved a sigh. He'd been trying to remain strong for Joanna's sake. Strong in hopes of helping her get through her grief. As if in mutual consent, they drew apart.

His gaze riveted on hers, compelling, silent. Feather-soft, he traced one finger down the side of her face and followed the delicate contours of her lips. Then he embraced her again, this time with unexpected urgency. In the space of a heartbeat, his mouth covered hers.

Delicious sensations assaulted her as she submitted to his kiss. She felt as if she were spiraling down into an endless black hole, faster, faster, into depths unknown. Instantly a familiar warning sprung to her mind. With a faint gasp, she broke the contact.

"What's the matter?" His words hung in the balance.

"I . . . we . . . this isn't right." She wrenched her gaze from his. She felt him regarding her for a long moment.

"Look at me," he said. "Please."

Hesitantly she lifted her gaze to his. His face was unreadable.

"I'm sorry. So sorry." Without a further word, he turned on his heel and strode out the front door.

***

Austin swerved the Jeep onto the highway, gripping the steering wheel till his hands ached. Overhead, gray clouds loomed. Rain hammered against the roof.

"What's come over me?" he muttered. He downshifted and peered at the glistening wet highway. He was playing with fire, he knew it. But being with Jo was almost more than he could bear.

Damn! If only she hadn't looked so irresistible, damp fluffs of baby-fine blond hair framing her gorgeous face, her blue eyes shining like sapphires. What red-blooded guy wouldn't have given in and kissed her—especially when he'd felt so vulnerable and empty.

Yep, there was no denying it. He'd needed to hold her close, kiss her long and tenderly, feel the comfort only she could give. And he'd sensed she needed that too. But it was scary, nearly driving him insane. Joanna was different than all the rest, and no matter how he tried to talk himself out of it, the truth was becoming plainly clear.

He slowed as he approached a hairpin turn, then remembered the wedding rings. How long had she been without them? Somehow he hadn't even noticed till today.

The rain slashed against the windshield as his thoughts raced on. He'd better keep himself in line. He was certainly no saint, and the last thing she needed was *him* complicating her life. Why did life have to be so complicated for both of them? Why couldn't she be anyone else than his deceased brother's wife?"

The white center line sped past like a never-ending kite string. The gray ribbon of highway stretched on and on. He wasn't sure where he was going. All he knew was he needed to keep driving. Maybe he should tell her the rest of his story. Maybe he should explain about his promise.

But on second thought, no, he decided. It wasn't necessary. She didn't need the details just yet. Besides, if she did know the truth, the *entire* truth, she'd tell him it was ridiculous and send him away. And that would make his guilt a hundred times greater. God only knew, it was tough enough dealing with it right now.

As he rounded the next curve in the highway, a new thought sprang to his mind. There was one way out, and only one way. He'd finish the repairs as fast as he could, then he'd hit the road again—due north, clean out of the country.

And if he was smart, he'd never look back.

***

Next evening, Joanna sauntered along the beach, cooling down after her daily run. That morning, for the first time since she'd moved to Southport, she'd overslept and missed it.

What on earth was happening to her? she wondered. Her usual discipline was dissolving like sugar in a cup of hot tea. If only she could get a decent night's sleep, perhaps she could get a better hold on herself.

Her moist T-shirt clung to her chest as she stepped over a gnarled piece of driftwood, then approached a larger log, where she finally sat down to think. From farther away, a curl of smoke from a beach fire rose lazily into the sky.

The earthy scent reached her, but it failed to evoke her usual enthusiasm. She picked up a pearly agate, turning it over methodically, feeling its smooth surfaces between her fingertips

What am I going to do? She had to admit she was falling hopelessly for Austin. He affected even the most routine aspects of her daily life. Sleep came with new difficulty, fraught with indecision, contrasting the depression-induced insomnia she'd experienced after Kyle died.

She was also consuming far too much caffeine. Picking at her food. Easily distracted on her job—a job she loved dearly. And every time Austin walked through her front door, her pulse raced.

She chewed on her lower lip. Which part of her would win out—her heart or her head?

No, it was definitely wrong to allow him to stay, but she couldn't bear for him to go. Not yet. She'd put it off for a while—at least till the roof was done. Then she'd somehow convince herself she could manage without him.

She stared out across the wave-tipped ocean and suppressed a shiver. It wasn't cold, really. In fact, until about an hour ago when the first clouds had swept in, it had been a warm, early October day, a spectacular play of gold and greens against a backdrop of blue. But at the aquarium while she'd been giving a slide show about marine ecosystems, she'd felt a chill and her head had throbbed unmercifully. Yes, she simply had to get a decent night's sleep, she reaffirmed, and as soon as she did, she'd be as good as new.

Shielding her eyes with her hand, she watched the sun sink behind the thickening bank of dark clouds that hugged the westernmost horizon. A gentle rain had begun to fall, a rain so fine one might disregard it completely.

"Sugar mist." The words formed softly on her lips, and she smiled. Yes, that's what the locals had always called it. *Sugar mist.* It smelled fresh and inviting, cooling her flushed cheeks, clinging gently to the tips of her eyelids. She inhaled deeply, squeezed her eyes shut, and savored the familiar old sensations from somewhere deep in her childhood.

Yet now the wind was rising, sweeping down the beach, whipping her hair about her face. From somewhere above, she heard the raucous screech of a crow. She rose and made her way to the water's edge, stepping over a translucent jellyfish that clung to the wet sand.

Tomorrow, she thought, staring up at the blustery sky. Tomorrow was the day of the beach cleanup and soon her long hours of preparation would be done. She'd checked out the beaches, the meeting and collection sites. The registration forms, data cards, and other supplies had arrived. And local service clubs had volunteered to provide lunches.

But even if Austin still intended to help—he hadn't mentioned it again for several days—she refused to allow his presence to sideline her. Yes, the preparations were nearly done, and for that she was grateful.

But the real work still lay ahead.

Chapter Five

The rain slanted down in wet ribbons of silver. The wind howled, rattling the windows. Though Austin had applied rain patches to the leaky spots on the roof as a temporary quick fix, one troublesome leak near Joanna's china hutch was worse than ever. Joanna had just emptied the pail beneath the leak. Now it was already half filled with new rainwater.

Joanna's shoulders slumped as she stared woodenly out the window. "What horrible timing," she said to Austin, turning around slowly to face him. She couldn't mask the despair in her voice. "A little while ago I was on the beach running, and except for a few dark clouds, the weather was fine."

He nodded. "Bad timing on two counts. Tomorrow morning's beach cleanup, plus your new roof. Now that the shingles have finally arrived and Trudy's husband is lined up to help on Sunday, this storm couldn't have happened at a worse time—"

". . . Seventy mile per hour winds and small craft warnings have been issued tonight on the Oregon coast and may last all weekend," the TV weather forecaster announced, slicing through Austin's next words. "Heavy rains could possibly lead to flooding and washed-out roads . . ."

Listening, they edged closer to the TV screen.

". . . Meanwhile, stay tuned for further developments in regards to the possible cancellation of tomorrow's Oregon Coast beach cleanup. Officials are conferring even as we speak. As I'm sure our viewing audience is well aware, safety is always first and foremost . . ."

"Those poor Boy Scouts," Joanna said. "I bet this is ruining their weekend camping trip too."

"If Camp Meriweather is anything like the one Kyle and I attended when we were kids, then there's most likely plenty of shelter," Austin answered. He cupped his hand beneath her elbow. "Dinner's getting cold. We can keep listening to the news while we eat."

"All right."

"Everything looks so elegant." She smiled at him, temporarily forgetting about the storm as she surveyed the spread of food he'd prepared: egg-plant casserole with three kinds of melted cheese, crusty French bread, romaine lettuce with endive salad, and chilled minted pears.

"Thanks. I've been slaving over a hot stove all day," he teased.

She could still feel where his touch had warmed her arm only a second ago—and fought off a new wash of desire. An hour earlier, she'd emerged from the shower and shrugged into a fresh T-shirt and her favorite black sweats while Austin set the table. It was obvious he'd gone to a great deal of trouble preparing this array of food. Though she still hadn't any appetite, she would simply have to try to eat.

"You know, it wasn't your turn to cook tonight," she reminded him as they took their seats facing each other. Though they'd agreed to share the dinner preparations—after all, two could eat more economically than one—his usual fare was sandwiches or heated canned soup and crackers. Yet Austin had cooked lavish meals like this the past three consecutive nights. And here he was again, eager and attentive, grinning like a proud schoolboy.

"Cooking was no trouble at all," he assured her. "But finding a tablecloth, now *that* was another story."

"What do you mean?"

One corner of his mouth turned up in a half smile. "I had to improvise. I picked a sheet out of your bathroom linen closet—the sheet still in the wrapper."

Her gaze dropped. Instantly she clapped her hand over her mouth at the sight of the floral pattern—a profusion of roses, mauves, and blue. She burst into laughter. "Oh, Austin, how clever! Of course, I don't mind. I don't mind at all. I don't have a matching sheet for this one anyway."

"I wanted to make tonight special," he continued. "You know, do away with the usual place mat and paper napkin routine. And as far as the wine glasses go, that part was easy. I spotted some in your china hutch a couple of weeks ago when I was painting."

"Oh!" A pang shot through her. She felt as if someone was sucking the air from her lungs. She hadn't even noticed the crystal goblets filled with white wine.

"What's the matter?" he asked. In the background, a blond news anchor was announcing the marriage of a famous sitcom actress.

Her voice was hushed. "The goblets were your wedding gift to us. The . . . the last time we used them was on our first anniversary."

His mouth dropped open. He dipped his head in embarrassment. "Oh, no. I thought for some reason they looked familiar." He suddenly stood up. "I'm sorry, Jo. What a stupid thing to do. Hold on. I'll find something else."

She fixed him with a meaningful look. "No. It's all right now. These goblets were Kyle's favorites." She swallowed hard as her eyes misted over. "I think he would be pleased." She hesitated. "Don't you?"

For a long moment Austin didn't answer, but instead sank back into his chair. A muscle in his jaw tensed. "Yes, I hope so." Then he lifted the wine glass, meeting her gaze over the rim. "To Kyle."

"Yes, to Kyle." Her eyes delved into his. The candlelight glimmered, illuminating the angles and plans of his too handsome face.

They shared the next moments in silence, but all the while, she couldn't deny her growing awareness of how powerfully his efforts had moved her. Elegant menu. The best white wine. His endearing attempts at procuring a tablecloth. And though the utilitarian white candle "centerpiece" looked like something he might have salvaged from the survival kit in his Jeep, she could've sworn it was the loveliest candle she'd ever seen.

"Italiano eggplant three cheese casserole is my forte," he announced, his tone lighter now. "You probably don't know this, but in my other life, I was a famous vegetarian chef."

"No, you don't say." She laughed giddily, allowing herself to indulge in this fleeting pleasure. All too soon she'd be sitting at this very table, solo again.

The thought snapped her back with a start. She hesitated, then shot him a direct look. "Why, Austin?"

"Why what?"

"Why are you doing all this?"

***

"I . . . I guess . . ." He shrugged with mock indifference. "Who knows? I always did sort of like to experiment in the kitchen."

He took another gulp of wine, tasted its fruity tartness, then swallowed audibly. Yeah. *Good question*, he thought. He knew his answer had sounded lame. Was the real reason merely to take care of her for Kyle's sake? Tempt her flagging appetite before she ended up getting sick? Or was it more . . . more than he was willing to admit to himself—or to her?

Outside, the wind blew harder, wailing like a lost child, nearly drowning out the voices on the TV. The chandelier above the table flickered, as did the television screen. Then the candle flame sputtered, and in a split second, puffed out.

"Some emergency candle," Austin said wryly. "I thought that wick looked a little too short."

She hopped up from her chair. "No problem. I'll go get more matches." In a few minutes she'd returned.

He got to his feet also. "I'll do that. You sit down and dig in before this food gets any colder."

She handed over the matches, then did as he'd said. Her headache had returned. The overhead chandelier was really much too bright.

She'd have to do something about that soon. Change the light bulbs, perhaps look for a dimmer switch.

She stabbed a lettuce leaf, then took a small bite, but each time she chewed, her head throbbed more. "Have I missed anything on the news?" she asked.

"No—nothing more about the beach cleanup, if that's what you mean." He glanced down at his watch. "National coverage starts in forty minutes, so I'm sure we'll hear an update before then."

She released a long, slow breath. "It's really a shame. After everyone's hard work and planning, there's a chance the event could be called off." Another chill rippled through her. It seemed every bone in her entire body ached too.

"Has it ever been canceled before?" Austin asked.

"Not that I know. Normally the cleanup takes place every fall and spring, rain or shine—though of course, unexpected storms always pose a threat." She took a small sip of wine to moisten her dry throat, then continued, "I'm worried that if the cleanup is canceled altogether and there isn't another one till next spring, that'll put even more marine wildlife at risk."

"Let's assume everything will still be on," he replied, biting into a chunk of eggplant. "The weather could change dramatically between now and tomorrow morning. And as for me, I'm hoping for clear skies so I can do some prep work on the roof before Grant Conner comes on Sunday."

She struggled to conceal her disappointment. How presumptuous of her to think that just because he'd assisted her with publicity, he intended to help with the actual cleanup too.

He slathered a slice of French bread with butter and asked, "By the way, speaking of tomorrow morning, what time do you have to report in? And where?"

She forced a smile. "The official starting time is ten. I need to arrive around eight to set up the coordination site in the parking lot at Two

Capes State Park. That's the one where the kids from the Boy Scout camp will meet, so I expect it's going to be especially busy."

"And if the cleanup's called off?"

"Then I'll have to go anyway. It's crucial that someone's there to turn away the folks who might've missed the announcement."

He must've noticed she had barely eaten her food, because he held his fork, in midair and asked, "What's the matter, Jo?"

"Nothing."

"I don't believe that." He studied her for a long moment. "You're sick, aren't you?"

"I'm fine." She sighed again and slanted him an apologetic look. "I'm sorry, Austin. This is such a lovely meal. It's just—"

"You can't fool me," he said, rising suddenly, moving to her side of the table. He held his hand on her forehead. "I may be a vet, but I can also tell when a member of the human species isn't well. You're running a fever. And your skin is pallid. Off to bed. Off right now. I'll get the aspirin and a glass of water."

"No, that's not necessary. It's nothing more than a little cold."

"Fine then. And the best cure for your little cold is bed rest. He scooped her up into his arms, his voice teasing, as he carried her away from the table. "Doctor's orders."

"No!" She struggled to get free, but he only clasped his arms more tightly around her. "Austin, please! Put me down. I'll rest on the sofa. It'll be better in no time."

He raised one eyebrow. "And you'll still take the aspirin?"

"Yes, Just put me down."

"All right then." His voice was firm, but gentle as he released her onto the thickly cushioned sofa and plumped up the oversize throw pillow behind her head and upper back. "There. Comfortable?"

"Yes. Very."

"Now just rest. I'll get you some juice and a blanket too. I won't be long."

She sighed, knowing he was right. Judging from the intensity of her chills, her fever was getting higher. But why? Why on the eve of the cleanup?

She lay there, propped against the pillow, half reclining, feet drawn up. As she stared absently at a dark speck on the ceiling, she heard Austin's footsteps retreating into the kitchen. Then came a thud as he opened a cupboard door, and the swish of running water at the kitchen sink.

She closed her eyes and lifted her fingertips to her temples in an attempt to still the pounding in her head. She had to admit it was nice having someone to pamper her right now. It seemed an eternity since she'd first found herself frightened and alone, then learned how to cope as a young widow—though barely. But Austin's stay was only temporary—and so was this virus, or whatever she'd picked up. Meanwhile, why not let him bring her aspirin and juice and a cozy blanket? Why not take refuge in his comforting presence when outside the wind was howling even louder, the rain pelting harder, like the flood for which Noah had built the ark.

"Whoa!" Austin's exclamation sounded from the laundry room, cutting through her muse. His deep laughter soon followed.

Her eyes flew open. "What happened?" she called. A blur of calico-colored fur whizzed in front of her, then vanished. Whatever it was, it must've startled the cat too.

Austin was still chuckling as he strode back into the room. "Does your cat always hide in the closet where you keep your extra blankets? I don't know who was more surprised, the cat or me?"

Joanna giggled sleepily, then yawned. "After seeing Silky streak by a second ago, I'd venture to say *she* was. And no, the only time she hides out like that is when good-looking strange men are lurking close by."

"Ah. So I see." He grinned crookedly as he shook out the blanket and tucked it around her then helped her sit up while she swallowed the medication. What a relief. At least she's still up to a little teasing, he struggled to reassure himself—but to no avail. Truth was, her skin felt even hotter than it had a few minutes ago and her eyes were now glazed with the fever.

"I'm so tired . . ." Her voice drifted off.

"Then sleep, Jo. I'll be right here if you need anything else."

Nodding, she closed her eyes.

He sat down on the empty spot at the end of the couch and hunched forward, his head in his hands. He'd heard a tough strain of flu would be prevalent this season, a flu that was often hard to lick and could lead to serious complications. If that's what was ailing Joanna, he might need to stick around even longer than he'd first planned.

He looked up, stared ahead unseeingly, and dragged a hand through his hair. How in good conscience could he leave her alone if she was still sick? And if this storm didn't let up and he couldn't get started on the roof this weekend, then that spelled double trouble. Damn! He was getting more locked in with each passing day.

"And now for the update about the Oregon Coast beach cleanup," the TV news announcer said, interrupting Austin's anxious thoughts. He straightened. Joanna opened her eyes and raised up on one elbow, leaning forward. "Officials from the Oregon State Parks Department and the U.S. Coast Guard have determined—"

The room went silent. The lights flicked off.

"Oh, no . . ." Joanna moaned. "What else can go wrong?"

"Do you have an old transistor radio?" Austin asked. Except for the faint glow of the candle on the dining room table, everything was black. "Most likely we can get the announcement on the radio, too," he added.

"I'm completely out of batteries. I meant to pick them up at the store, but I forgot." She sat up. "Maybe I should go out and get some."

"No, that's ridiculous. Not in your condition. Besides, I don't think it's wise for either of us right now. There could be power lines down too. And you know what they said about the roads flooding."

She yawned again, lying back down. There was no use arguing. His reminder made good sense. What was more, she'd almost fallen asleep.

She felt the sofa sag as he shifted his weight. "What about Trudy?" he asked. "She's probably listening to the news right now too. I should call her."

"Good idea. Her number's on my cell phone." She pointed to her phone on the coffee table. "Probably wouldn't hurt to call Aunt Marcella also and make sure everything's all right. There are some tall evergreens growing close to her house. A wind like this could easily take one down."

Sometime later—she was too drowsy to know exactly when—he'd returned from the kitchen where he'd tried to place the calls.

"More bad news," he said. His voice barely penetrated her fog. "Apparently the cell reception is down. I couldn't get through."

"Hmmm . . ." She felt his hand on her forehead again.

He tucked the blanket more snugly around her. "No matter. No matter now," he said in an infinitely tender voice. "Your fever's coming down. That's what's most important now."

He was near. Very near. Perhaps he'd drawn up a chair, or was sitting on the floor alongside her.

"'Night, Austin."

"Rest well, Jo . . ."

She felt him stroke back her hair, his touch feather-light. Then he pressed her knuckles against his lips as she slipped into a warm, fuzzy sleep.

***

Joanna stretched stiffly and coughed. A ribbon of daylight fell beneath her bedroom curtains, showing the first traces of a soft gray dawn. It sounded as if the rain had stopped. Against her feet she felt a familiar cat size weight, and heard Silky's purring.

She rolled over to one side. The digital clock flashed on and off. She blinked twice and looked down. She was still wearing her T-shirt and sweats. How did she get here? Hadn't Austin left her last night bedded down on the couch? Wherever she'd slept, all she remembered was that she'd tossed restlessly all night long.

She felt exhausted. Drained. And though her headache had improved some, her muscles still ached. She coughed again, this time harder.

"Good morning, sleeping beauty!" Austin poked his head in through the opened door. He put on a broad smile that belied his gnawing concern. "I thought I heard you stirring."

"Hi. When did you come back?"

As he took a couple of steps closer, Silky opened one cautious amber eye and held her gaze steadily on him.

"Actually, I never left," he replied.

"Oh?"

"After you fell asleep on the couch, I sat there with you for a while, waiting to see what was going to happen with the weather. But you didn't appear comfortable, so I carried you in here."

"And you stayed here all night?"

He hesitated. "I . . . I didn't want to leave you alone. I slept on the sofa."

She slid to the edge of the bed, planted her feet on the ground, but her knees felt wobbly. She started to sway. "W—what time is it? Are the phones working now? Have you tried to call Trudy?"

"It's six-fifteen and time you got right back in bed. And yes, I phoned Trudy. Ted Ashelman too."

"And?"

His hand was firm on her shoulder. "I'll tell you after you get back into bed."

"Oh, all right!" she huffed weakly. Why did he insist on bribing her like this? Couldn't he see she was perfectly capable of resuming her normal activities?

Reluctantly, she crawled back beneath the covers. Austin sat on the side of the bed. An apparently annoyed Silky leapt down, then disappeared.

"The rain stopped shortly after midnight," he explained, "so there was no flooding as previously expected. The winds died down around that time also."

"So the beach cleanup's still on?"

"Yes. According to Trudy, the announcement we missed last night said the decision would be postponed till the early morning hours. I've been listening to the radio since five, and the event is definitely going to happen."

"Terrific!" Her spirits soared. "Didn't you say it's a little after six? That gives me less than two hours to get ready . . ."

"I don't think that's a good idea."

"But why not? I'm fine now. Perfectly—" She stopped short, coughing. This time the cough wracked her entire body.

He handed her a glass of water and she accepted it gratefully.

The coughing stopped.

"Listen, Jo," Austin said, taking her hand in his, working his thumb gently across her palm. "There's nothing to worry about. I've got everything under control. I told Trudy I'd man your coordination site and do all the other things you were supposed to do. Ted is going to help and he'll fill me in on the details. He's worked at other cleanups and was planning on pitching in anyway."

She smiled at him, overcome with mixed emotions. Relief that the storm had stopped. Gratitude for his willingness to take over. And bitter disappointment that she would have to miss out.

"All right," she murmured, resigned at last. "I . . . I guess it would be foolish of me to try to go."

"That's more like it." He squeezed her hand and returned her smile. "Austin?"

"Yes, Jo?"

"One more thing. I . . . I want to say thanks." She chewed on her lower lip, remembering how eager he'd been to work on the roof. "You really didn't have to. I mean, I'm sure we could find someone else who'd be willing to step in."

"How could I not want to help when I know how much it means to you?"

Chapter Six

"Look, pal. Last night's storm only proved my point. Weather here on the coast can be fickle." Ted Ashelman shot Austin a direct look as he ripped open a large cardboard box. "You're gonna need extra help to get the roof on as fast as possible. I'll come tomorrow at six."

After arriving at Two Capes State Park and proceeding to the group picnic shelter, the men now busied themselves setting out registration forms, data collection cards, plastic bags, and disposable gloves. Only minutes earlier, Austin had explained about Grant Conner's offer to help with the roof.

"Thanks, Ted," Austin said, "but I can't let you."

"Why not?"

"You need your time off—probably even more than a vet at an average clinic does." Austin lifted a beach safety poster and tacked it to the information board behind the registration table.

"Way I see it, one good turn deserves another," Ted said with a shrug. "You helped me at Anchorhold. I'll help you and Conner with the roof. The three of us, we should get the work done in no time." A seagull swooped down onto the picnic shelter railing and cocked its head as it regarded the men curiously.

"You know Conner?"

"Yeah. Small town, don't forget." The older man chuckled. "Makes a guy keep his nose clean. Anyway, Conner helped my wife and me sell our home over on Twenty-third Street. He's top-notch in everything he does—but no matter how you slice it, three can get that roof on faster than two."

"I guess I can't argue about that," Austin said, his voice tentative.

"You like shellfish, Sullivan? Maybe afterwards we can all get together at my place for a clambake. I went out at the crack of dawn this morning and got my limit."

"Well, all right. But we may have to take a rain check." Austin inhaled deeply as his gaze swept the parking lot that fronted the day use area. The rain-washed air held a faint odor of damp humus mingled with the tangy smell of salt water. An assortment of tree branches, remnants from last night's storm, lay scattered about. Already the sun was getting hot, causing a light mist to rise from the pavement.

"Why put the roof off?" Ted scratched the bald spot on the back of his head. "I thought you said the shingles finally came in."

"They did. But now there's another problem." Austin aligned a row of pencils with deliberate precision as if trying to get his ducks in order.

"What kind of problem?"

"It's Jo."

"Joanna?"

"Yes. In fact, I kind of hated leaving her for so long today, but it was the only way I could keep her from insisting on being here herself."

"She's pretty sick, huh?"

"Yeah, that new strain of flu, I think. She's spiking a high fever, has a dry cough, and has been battling some killer headaches." He squared his jaw, then frowned. "The last thing she needs is us pounding overhead."

"Good point. Hey, look. I can manage alone if you think you should go." Ted nodded to his cell phone. "I can always ring up someone else to give me a hand."

"I . . . I'm not sure exactly what I should do, but I promised her I'd take her place today. If I don't stick to it, she may jolly well drive right over here—fever, cough, and all. It's the only way I can keep her down."

"Oh, I see. The independent type . . . just like my missus." One corner of Ted's mouth lifted. "Now why doesn't that surprise me?" He rocked back on his heels and hitched his thumbs in his belt loops. "Well, as far as the roof goes, just let me know. We'll work it in—whenever. I hope the little lady is back on her feet soon."

"So do I. And thanks. Thanks again, Ted." Though Austin's voice was filled with appreciation, he couldn't dismiss how the tenor of their conversation was frightening him. It seemed they were talking almost as if he and Jo were husband and wife. He had to change the subject. He had to change it quickly. "By the way, any further news about the owl Joanna hauled into Anchorhold?"

"It recovered without incident. I turned the owl loose not far from her place."

"Good, I'll tell her. That should help pick up her spirits." Austin lifted the collar of his windbreaker against the rising breeze.

Ted grinned. "You're too late, pal. She already knows. She phoned in to check on the owl almost every day."

"I might've guessed," Austin answered with a chuckle. "Pretty soon, she'll probably be showing up on your doorstep to be your newest volunteer."

"You're too late on that one also. She said she's making arrangements at the aquarium to take off every Friday afternoon so she can help me. It might take her another few weeks to get everything squared away, but she's working on it."

"And by that time, if I'm lucky, I'll be well on my way up north," Austin said. "I'll be holed up in some fishing shack, living the good life." He rummaged through a box in search of the extra bag ties, then glanced at his watch. Hopefully the local service club would show up in time to dish out the traditional picnic lunch, he thought anxiously. If he and Ted had to take charge of that, too, those poor volunteers might starve.

"You in a hurry to leave Southport?" the older man asked, snapping Austin back from his thoughts.

"Yep."

"Why?"

"I'm just Jo's hired help—even though I'm her late husband's brother." Austin hesitated, realizing that Ted undoubtedly knew little, if any, of the circumstances. He told him briefly, then added, "To make matters even stickier, I'm practically the spitting image of Kyle—and because of that, it's tough on Jo. She needs to get on with her life without my complicating it."

"And how do you feel about all this?"

"Austin swiped a hand over his chin and sighed. "I knew you'd ask." He paused. "Okay, here goes. Bottom line is, I'm not sure how much longer I can hang in there, living so close to her like this. Besides, it's a guy thing, you know? I'd never take advantage of Jo—emotionally or otherwise." Absently he brushed sand off the registration table.

Ted nodded. "I'm sorry about your brother. Real sorry. And I read you, pal. You'd have to be blind, and probably half dead too, not to realize what a looker Joanna is."

"Yeah, and not only that. She's caring, dedicated, intelligent." His voice caught. "I've never known anyone quite like her."

For the next half hour they continued working, tacking up more posters, answering questions from inquisitive campers, and taking final inventory on registration supplies. All the while, they chatted companionably.

Maybe this is what I've been missing back home, Austin thought. The small-town camaraderie. Friends helping friends. Handshakes and clambakes instead of corporate back-stabbing and cocktail parties. In some ways, perhaps, it was a shame he hadn't any intentions of staying around. Then too, he'd really taken a liking to Ted Ashelman.

Austin looked down at his watch again. "I'm getting nervous, Ted."

"Why? You have an aversion to crowds or something?"

"No. It's the hot dog feed that's got me concerned. Where's the service club that's supposed to handle it?"

"Uh-oh." Ted's face fell. "I almost forgot. You're right, Sullivan. The Lions Club. They were due almost an hour ago with Jake's Wiener Wagon. They're normally as reliable as the sun and the moon. If they haven't shown by now, then there must be something wrong."

The jangle of his cell phone sliced through his next words.

"What? Speak louder, Jake! Our connection's lousy."

While Ted talked, Austin watched a shadow pass across the older man's face. "You sure there's no other way? Isn't there someone else who could bring in the supplies?" A long pause followed. "Oh, I see. Well, thanks for the call. Looks as if we'll have to forget it this time."

"We've got a problem," Ted explained, turning to Austin after he'd folded up the phone. "Jake was about ten miles down the highway when he called. The Wiener Wagon got stopped by a major mudslide that's blocking both lanes of 101. Jake had no other choice but to turn back. No one's been injured, thankfully, but there's going to be big-time delays. It's right near the tunnel on the north end of town."

"And there's no one else who can fill in?"

"Apparently not. Jake tried calling other club members, but they were either not home, or already involved at other registration sites."

Austin heaved a sigh. "Now what? The hot dog feed has been highly publicized. It's part of the incentive to get people to turn out."

"True enough, but don't overlook the obvious, Sullivan. If Jake can't get through, then that's probably also true for many of the volunteers."

"But what about the Boy Scout camp?" Austin countered. "Joanna worked especially hard to solicit their help. It'd really be a shame to let those kids down."

"Oh, wow." Ted's faced paled. "I forgot about that. Maybe I could call my wife or—"

"No, don't bother," Austin cut him off. "I'll go round up the food. You man the registration table." His mind raced as he scanned the picnic shelter. "I see there are built-in barbecues," he said, "but we'll need several bags of charcoal. Is there a store close by? I'll buy a couple dozen packages of hot dogs and a ton of potato salad and soda pop and—"

Before Ted could answer, the sound of an approaching van interrupted their conversation. Behind it droned a smaller van, followed by a meandering string of other vehicles. In seconds, doors were slamming, kids were running towards them, shrieking with laughter.

"The Boy Scouts! Not already!" Austin let out a low moan.

Ted chuckled. "It looks as if we underestimated. Forget the couple dozen packages of hot dogs, pal. You'd better get a couple hundred."

***

Three hours later, the aroma of sizzling frankfurters wafted on the early afternoon breeze as boys of all ages waited eagerly off to the side, paper plates in hand, while others sat eating at picnic tables. The din of their conversation was punctuated with bursts of laughter. Meanwhile, other volunteers had begun to filter inside the picnic shelter, some in couples, and others in small groups. Obviously the washed-out highway hadn't deterred everyone.

"You saved the day," Ted Ashelman muttered under his breath. The men stood hunkered over two barbecues, waiting for the next round of hot dogs to finish cooking. Joe Oretega, district Scout coordinator, had also pitched in and was dishing out potato salad and chips, while his wife, Clara, passed out the buns and soft drinks.

"No, *you* did, Ashelman," Austin tossed back modestly, though the look on his face reflected his own sense of relief. "You stayed here alone and got these kids all registered and organized while all I had to do was go shopping. If you asked me, I got the easy end of that deal."

"Don't try to fool me. You were sweating bullets there for awhile, and you know it." Ted's mouth quirked in a smile. "Matter of fact, I guess we both were. But what the heck? We pulled it off anyway."

"And judging from the volunteers' comments on their data cards," Austin pointed out, "plus the number of filled bags we put in the parking lot dumpster, the event was a huge success."

Austin eyed the wieners, roasted and bubbling, then called. "Come and get 'em, everyone! Line forms to the right. I'm getting pretty good at the cooking bit," he added to Ted, then laughed. "But don't tell that to Joanna. She might not approve of hot dogs."

"I hope you hung onto your grocery receipts," Ted said as a swarm of boys rushed back for seconds. "The Lions Club will want to reimburse you."

"No big hurry."

"Oh? You playing hero or what? I thought you said it won't be long till you're out of here." Ted slanted him a questioning look as he plopped two wieners on the first boy's plate.

Austin shrugged with forced indifference. "That's what I'd like, but that's not necessarily what I'll get. It all depends on the roof and how quickly Jo recovers, don't forget."

Yet do I really want to leave? Wouldn't a few more weeks with Joanna be just as good as a fishing trip? Maybe even better?

***

"Don't worry, Aunt Marcella. I'll be up and running in no time—tomorrow morning at the latest." That afternoon, Joanna sat propped up in bed, her cell phone pressed to her ear. "Austin was just overreacting when he insisted I stay home from the beach cleanup, but I somehow let him talk me into it." She coughed, then continued.

"So how are you? Did you lose your power last night? Are all your trees still standing?"

"Heavens, I'm afraid I slept through the whole thing. I didn't even realize there were high winds till I listened to the television this morning." Marcella's laughter rippled brightly on the other end of the line. "And yes, the trees are fine. Standin' green and tall and ramrod-straight."

"Good. I meant to call earlier but . . ." Joanna's voice drifted off as she wracked her mind for a plausible excuse. She was reluctant to admit she'd been drowsy most of the day and was still feeling as if she'd been run over by a dune buggy. There was no point in worrying Aunt Marcella unnecessarily. Besides, she would be as good as new tomorrow.

"Now, Jo, you do take care of yourself," Marcella said. "Remember to drink plenty of hot tea to soothe that cough. And please give my love to Austin. It was so good of him to take over for you. Yes, he's a mighty good man."

"Oh, there's Austin right now," Joanna said. "I hear his Jeep pulling into the driveway."

"Then I'll let you go."

"Take care of yourself, too, Aunt Marcella." She coughed again and blew her nose into a tissue. "And don't hesitate to call if you need anything—I'm sure I'm not contagious anymore."

"Don't worry, dear. You know perfectly well my next-door neighbor, Lucille, checks in twice a day. Now snuggle back down in bed so you don't take another chill."

"I will. Bye."

Austin appeared in the doorway, both arms behind his back. Though his hair was slightly mussed and his shirt wrinkled, he wore a self-satisfied look on his face. "How's my favorite sister-in-law?" he asked.

"Better, thanks." She swallowed to stifle another cough.

"Good." Eyes shining, he held out a profuse bouquet of lemony yellow roses.

"Oh, Austin! They're beautiful." She took them from his outstretched arms and buried her nose in the fragrant, soft petals.

"I drove by the florist's shop on my way home . . . and . . . well." He shrugged. "I couldn't resist. I thought you might need a little cheering up. Besides, I used to grow roses a lot like these—back in the days when I had time for gardening."

"There's a vase in the utility room, on the top shelf," she said, visibly touched as she handed back the bouquet. It seemed forever since she had arranged cut flowers to brighten her home, but then this past year here entire life had been pretty colorless too.

"Fine. I'll go get these in some water," he said, holding the roses out at arm's length again, eyeing them with a pleased expression.

In minutes, he'd returned. He set the bouquet down on her bedside table. For a long moment, his eyes held hers.

"Thank you," she said in barely a whisper. "I thought about you all day, you know. I kept trying to imagine you there at the registration site, wondering how you were getting along."

He sat down on the side of her bed and took her hand in his. "So you want to hear all the grizzly details?"

"Of course!"

"Well, for starters, Ted and I saved two hundred-plus Boy Scouts from the clutches of starvation."

"What?"

"Uh-huh. Yours truly managed to pull off his culinary genius once again—thanks to Ted's help, of course." His face was wreathed in a smile as he proceeded to explain what had happened. "You should've seen Ted and me, trying to keep cool while we were mobbed by all those hungry kids."

She giggled. "If I'd only known, I would've dragged myself out of bed and driven right over there."

"To rescue me, or watch me flounder?"

"Maybe a little of both."

"Seriously though, I think the cleanup was a huge success," Austin continued. "Of course, we'll know more when all the results are in. If the other beaches produced even half as much refuse as Two Capes did, then I'd say we'd put a big dent in the problem."

"So what sort of stuff did people find?" she asked.

"Most was plastic, as we already expected. Vegetable sacks, sheeting, meat trays, bottles, diapers, six-pack rings, that sort of thing. Among the nonplastics, there were shoes, light bulbs, beverage cans, even crab traps." His eyes crinkled at the corners. "One woman told us how she and her friend struggled with a sheet of plastic that was poking up through the sand below a large dune. They tugged and tugged, puzzled at why it should be so firmly rooted—until they finally looked up and discovered the reason. The plastic was not the small piece they had originally thought. Although part of it was buried where they were standing, the rest was covering the entire dune. It'd been put there to protect the dune from erosion!"

"I bet that's not the first time that happened," Joanna said after they'd shared a chuckle. Her thoughts rolled back to the beached sea lion she'd found that first day Austin had made his unannounced visit. "Did anyone find any more dead or injured animals that had been trapped by debris?"

"Sorry to say, there were several dead seagulls, though as you know, the volunteers were instructed to leave them on the beach. None of the gulls appeared entangled though."

"I'm glad," she replied.

"Some of the folks I talked to estimated the number of six-pack rings collected were much less than last year. Apparently the word's getting out. People are remembering to cut through the rings, so that they can't pose a danger to the animals."

They talked on and on, till Joanna's voice had grown so raspy Austin insisted it was time for him to leave. "I'll be close by, most likely in the kitchen, painting the trim strip above the cupboards," he said. "But first, would you like me to bring you anything? Some soup and crackers? A cup of tea?"

"No thanks. I already fixed myself a cheese sandwich shortly before you arrived." Drowsy again, she shut her eyes. It felt so good to simply lay still and rest. Their talking had tired her more than she'd realized.

She could hear the sound of his footfall grow softer, then finally fade down the hallway. The heady perfume of the roses drifted her way and she smiled, recalling the look on Austin's face when he'd given them to her. Roses. Soft yellow roses. Had he known they'd always been her favorite?

She must've dozed for nearly an hour, because when she awoke, the late-afternoon shadows had grown more angular, the sunlight dimmer.

Yet the sound of Austin talking jolted her to her senses.

She sat up, straining to hear.

"Oh, no. Just stay right where you are," he was saying, his voice tight. "I'll be right over."

Chapter Seven

"What's wrong?" Joanna called to Austin.

"That was Marcella," he answered in a rush, appearing again in the doorway. "She's taken a fall. Says not to worry, she's fine. She just needs help getting back on her feet."

"Did she trip? Have a dizzy spell?" Joanna's chest tightened with apprehension. It was just like her aunt to downplay a potentially serious situation. Marcella never wanted anyone to fuss over her.

"She didn't say. Gotta hurry!" Austin jangled his key chain impatiently. "I'll fill you in when I get back." Flashing her a guarded smile, he turned on his heel and disappeared.

Joanna's heart hammered as she listened to the roar of his Jeep fading down the highway. She prayed Aunt Marcella was all right. But what if a stroke or heart attack had precipitated her fall? What if she'd fractured a hip? Joanna blinked with disbelief. Why, only a few hours earlier, they'd visited on the phone, comparing notes about the night's storm, sharing a laugh or two. If her aunt hadn't been feeling well, she'd certainly managed to fool Joanna.

Fretful, Joanna got to her feet, put on her slippers, and shrugged into her white terry bathrobe. She couldn't just stay in bed . . . she had to do something.

Padding down the hallway, she wandered into the front room and peered through the opened blinds that covered the picture window. Austin had left the window ajar a few inches. A brisk breezed caused the blinds to clatter against the sill. Behind her, the floor lamp, next to the overstuffed chair where Silky snoozed, cast a rosy glow.

Outside, the purple dusk was growing deeper. To her right, a streetlight illuminated her front yard, the juniper hedge, the wheelbarrow Austin had left on the lawn before he'd decided to postpone his prep work on the roof. From the front street, car headlights cut swathes through the darkness. Mr. Peabody, the neighbor next door, turned into his driveway, then turned off the engine of his SUV.

Suppressing a shiver, Joanna hugged her arms to her chest. She thought again about Aunt Marcella.

And Kyle.

How, in only a split moment, could one's life change so drastically—and as in Kyle's case, come to an abrupt end?

Kyle. In the stillness of the empty house, her thoughts rolled back to their wedding day. A day bathed in sunlight and laughter. How handsome Kyle had looked, how magnificently robust and alive, his face bronzed by the early summer sun, his eyes bright with happiness.

She'd been so ecstatic, so blissfully in love, she'd scarcely cast a second glance, figuratively speaking, at any other man who'd come to witness their vows. Even Austin.

Oh, yes, there had been the hearty handclasps and tearful hugs. But somehow the two brothers' uncanny resemblance had never struck her—not even at the time of the funeral, eighteen months later. Of course, her awareness had not been altered only by her love for her deceased husband, but also by her indescribable grief. How could she have dreamed that in still another twelve months, Austin's presence would be tearing her resolve into a thousand shreds?

She turned away from the window and bit her lower lip. Unbidden, the years stretched before her, like solitary building blocks winding into some nebulous future. And what exactly would that future hold in store? she asked herself. Would she remain alone, forever looking back? Did she dare dream of a life with Kyle's older brother?

She pulled her thoughts back to the present. Surely Austin must have arrived at Marcella's by now. Hopefully he'd find her every bit as alert and coherent as when she'd phoned. Hopefully, somehow, she'd escaped from harm's way. *Well, as the old saying goes,* Joanna reminded herself, *no news is good news.*

The phone rang again, giving Joanna a start. Checking the caller ID and realizing it was Austin, she fumbled to answer it. *So much for the no news bit.*

"Oh, Austin! How's Auntie?" She swallowed hard to keep from coughing.

"As far as I can tell, nothing's broken, but she does have a good-sized lump on her head from where she hit the coffee table on her way down. Her vital signs are okay, but I'm concerned about a possible concussion. I'm taking her to the ER right away."

"Oh . . . yes. By all means . . ." She pressed a hand to her heart. "And Austin?"

"Yes, Jo?"

"Call me again as soon as you know more, will you?"

"Of course."

To fill the anxious moments, Joanna wandered into the kitchen and began loading the dishwasher. Then, feeling a bit shaky, she heated a kettle of water and fixed a cup of mint tea. The tea would not only calm her nerves, but help the congestion in her chest, she decided.

Meanwhile, the phone rang three more times, the first, a wrong number, the other two, calls from solicitors. *Whatever is taking Austin so long?* she fretted as she carried her teacup back to the living room and sat down. It seemed an eternity till the next call came through.

"Hi!" Austin's voice boomed again on the other end. This time he sounded more composed. "Sorry it took so long, but what with the paperwork and—"

"How is she?" Joanna interrupted.

"Complaining of a headache, but otherwise all right—for now at least. Your aunt told me while we were waiting to be seen that she tripped on the area rug in her dining room, and that's what caused her fall."

"Oh, dear. I warned her about that."

"The ER doctor agreed there's danger of a possible concussion," Austin hurried on. "Marcella shouldn't be alone. The only way I could keep him from admitting her was to assure him she wouldn't be. I'm going to stay with her tonight and maybe part of tomorrow. We'll see how it goes. That'll also give me a chance to remove that rug before she trips on it again."

"Why don't we put her up in the guest room? Like I said I'm almost as good as new, so I should be able to help take care of her. Besides, the new dusty rose comforter I put on the bed is just begging for someone to use it."

"I'm not sure that would be a good idea. Regardless of what you say, you're still pretty sick. At Marcella's age, catching the flu could prove serious."

"But I am better. A lot better. Aunty will never hear of your playing nursemaid to her. She's too proud. She'll insist she can manage by herself."

"Proud?" His voice hinted at his amusement.

"All right. Stubborn, then." She coughed. "You might say it runs in the family."

"I know, Jo." He chuckled good-naturedly. "How well I know."

Ignoring his remark, Joanna continued. "One more thing."

"Yes?"

"Don't forget Marcella's next-door neighbor, the one who checks in twice a day. Lucille Shores, I think her name is. She needs to be notified as soon as possible. I'm afraid, though, I don't have her number. If Auntie isn't hurting too badly, maybe she can remember."

"Lucille's gone," he said.

"What?"

"I said Lucille's gone."

"What do you mean, *gone*?" Joanna's voice rose with controlled panic. "I talked to Auntie only a few hours ago. She assured me that Lucille was close at hand."

"According to Marcella, soon after you phoned her, Lucille stopped by. She had just learned that her daughter in St. Louis was undergoing emergency abdominal surgery. She's a single mom with four little kids all under the age of seven. Lucille is planning to stay with them till everything's back under control."

He lowered his voice. Joanna could almost see him tossing a wary glance over his shoulder to see whether Auntie was eavesdropping. "Marcella figured that wouldn't be a problem. She thought by the time she'd need groceries or a ride to the doctor's, you'd be well again. Meanwhile she wasn't going to let on about Lucille's leaving till it was absolutely necessary."

"That sounds like Aunt Marcella. Well, at any rate, we know now." Joanna sighed deeply. "Drive safely. The weather forecast predicts heavy fog tonight. And please give my love to Auntie."

"I will."

Back at Marcella's home, she and Austin stood talking in the narrow hallway next to her bedroom. Penlight in hand, he reminded her he would be coming in very hour to check her pupils and determine her level of consciousness. Though at first she protested vehemently, now the gratitude was written clearly on her face.

"Such a fuss over an old lady like me," she said as she held an ice pack to her head. "But what a gentleman you are." She smiled and patted his cheek with her other hand. "Just think, my own private doctor—an animal doctor, at that. My hubby always said if his life was ever at stake, he'd choose an animal doctor over a people doctor every time."

"At your beck and call, Aunt Marcella." He smiled back and gave her a mock salute. Then his expression sobered. "Seriously, though, I'm glad I can help. It's given us an excuse to get to know each other better. Besides, I never had an aunt. Jo's lucky."

"And likewise, I've never had a nephew. Nieces. All six of 'em." She chuckled. "Nothin' but Barbie dolls and tea parties." She turned to the bedroom. "Goodnight, Mr. Sullivan."

"Goodnight." He paused. "And Aunt Marcella?"

"Yes?" She turned her head stiffly.

"Please call me Austin."

"Fine then. Austin it is."

He broke into a lopsided smile. And one more thing . . ." He paused, his smile widening.

"Go on," she urged.

"Better get right to sleep. I'll see you again in exactly an hour."

A short time later, Austin struck a match to the kindling, split logs, and crumpled newspaper he'd arranged in the stone fireplace. Joanna had been right about the weather. Later that evening, thick fog had blanketed the coast, and now the house felt damp and chilly. He'd also noted this past week that the vine maple was beginning to turn. All that added up to one disturbing reality. Autumn was definitely in full bloom—and the fish up north were probably biting like crazy.

He sank down into Marcella's blue recliner that faced the fireplace, and stared into the dancing orange-red flames. Though the leather was worn and cracked, it felt familiar and comfortable—like a favorite old glove one hated to throw away.

His thoughts turned back to the day he and Jo had shared their first kiss—the sensual feeling of her lips pressed against his, her quickening heartbeat against his chest. How he longed to hold her again, to trail small kisses down her cheeks and whisper sweet words into her ears. But then she'd taken ill, and he'd given her the space she needed to recover despite his own desires. That's what was the most important for now, right? But how much longer would he have to wait?

Stretching out his long legs, he heaved a sigh. His morning had started at the crack of dawn when he'd first received the news that the beach cleanup was still on. After that, one near catastrophe had given away to the next.

He was tired. Damn. Sheer exhaustion was more like it. And he'd be getting little sleep in the hours that lay ahead. Not that he was complaining, exactly, he silently amended as he leaned back farther in the chair and listened to the fire crackle and pop. Somehow—and it was downright scary—it felt good to be needed. It felt good to realize there might be someone who noticed your coming and going, that you weren't merely an isolated nonentity in this crazy, fast-paced world.

But now two females depending on him? Unbelievable!

He clasped his hands behind his neck, then chuckled in spite of himself. Yes, that's what it was going to take to get him through. A sense of humor. Never in a million years would he have fathomed he'd get sidelined like this.

Good thing it was only temporary, or was it? He was beginning to wonder if the end would ever come. It looked as if he'd be putting off that new roof for at least another week, if not longer, till Jo fully recovered. And now there was Aunt Marcella. He squared his jaw. Bottom line was, she required his help too.

***

The following week ticked slowly by. Aunt Marcella recovered without incident, though Austin checked in on her faithfully twice a day. Sometimes he picked up her medicine, sometimes a bag of groceries. And sometimes he simply stayed to talk.

Meanwhile, Joanna was making her own slow recovery. Her cough finally began to subside, and the rosy blush in her cheeks reappeared.

Yet, in between running errands for Marcella, Austin continued to keep a watchful eye over Joanna. His concern touched Joanna in ways she'd never expected. Her feelings for him had only grown deeper—and a thousand times more chaotic.

"What are you doing?" Austin asked the following Saturday morning when she appeared in the dining room dressed in a pale blue running suit. He was sitting at the breakfast nook table, reading the newspaper and drinking coffee.

"I'm going for a run. I've been cooped up inside for far too long!" she exclaimed.

"Whoa! Just one minute." He clasped a restraining hand on her shoulder.

"Just one minute *what*?" she protested. "I'm going crazy!"

"I understand, Jo. But you know as well as I do, you've got to ease back into your routine gradually. "You're probably still weak—and prone to a relapse."

"I'm fine now. Besides, I told Trudy I'd be back to work on Monday. It's also high time I started helping Auntie. I can't expect you to keep doing that—especially when we need to get the roof on as soon as possible."

He stroked his chin. She was right about that much. The bundles of shingles he'd stacked in the carport a week ago still lay unopened, and he'd grown more frustrated every time he'd spied them.

"All right. Just take it easy, okay? I'll keep breakfast warm till you get back."

Her lips parted in a saucy smile. "I'll make you a deal. I won't run today—or the rest of the week either. I'll just take a walk. Nothing more."

"Promise?"

"Scout's honor."

"Mind if I walk with you?"

"Of course not. But just don't worry so. I'm going to be fine."

"Of course you are. I guess I've been so busy playing doctor to you and Marcella, I haven't had the good sense to know when to stop." He darted her a contrite smile. "Sorry, Jo."

"Don't apologize. Your help has been a godsend, believe me. Taking over at the beach cleanup. Helping with Auntie. Cooking my meals." She hesitated. "And most of all, bringing me yellow roses."

An hour later, they strolled hand-in-hand down the beach. A lazy sun shed its soft milky light as it filtered through the mist rising up from the water. The breeze nipped their cheeks and tousled their hair.

Throngs of others had flocked there also—undoubtedly in an attempt to capture the last beautiful days of autumn. Teenagers threw Frisbees. Dogs barked. Children with plastic buckets filled with water knelt as they built sand castles. Overhead, an assortment of brightly-colored kites drifted on the wind.

Austin let go of her hand, then stooped to pick up a flat gray rock. He pitched it far into the ocean. They watched it plunge below the blue-gray depths.

"Ah! Not bad," he said with a laugh. "I haven't done that since I was a kid." He caught her hand again and gave it a quick squeeze.

"Everything's so beautiful!" Joanna exclaimed, filling her lungs with the tangy salt air. "One week indoors, and I feel as if I've been away from this forever." Today, for some reason, the sea appeared more translucent. The sand whiter. The sky a thousand times bluer.

Was it merely her confinement that had sharpened her senses so? Or this wonderful, caring man striding close by her side? The thought caught her suddenly off guard, making her heart turn over."

"Ah, Jo. You should've been a mermaid." He angled her a look, then paused, his eyes teasing. "If I remember my Greek mythology correctly," he went on, "the mermaids' singing lured many a sailor. And the German story of the nymph Lorelei says she inhabited a cliff overlooking the Rhine."

"And if I'm remembering right," she teased back, "Lorelei turned out to also be the poor sailors' undoing. She beckoned them to the rocks below. She caused their destruction."

He chuckled. "But isn't that the destiny of every unfortunate man who falls beneath the wiles of an alluring female?"

She pulled her eyes from his, wondering whether his statement carried some hidden agenda. She had to ask. "And that's why, Austin Sullivan, in all your thirty-one years, you've made sure to stay single? To escape such destruction?"

"Perhaps. But don't knock bachelorhood." The mirth vanished from his face. "There's something to be said for going it alone."

He balled his hand into a fist, his thoughts spinning. What that something was, he could no longer be sure—but he'd be damned if he'd admit that to her. Besides, he'd soon be gone, and so much the better. These past weeks had tested his restraint in ways he'd never anticipated.

They walked on in silence, listening to the gentle hiss of the surf licking the shore. Straight ahead, Cape Castaway jutted out. In minutes, they approached a small deserted cove and stopped to gaze at a rocky precipice where, at the bottom, russet-colored starfish clung. The cliff, deeply chiseled and glistening with sea spray, loomed high above them.

"Let's sit down," Austin suggested, nodding towards a sun-bleached log.

"Good idea. I guess you were right. I'm tiring a little more quickly than I expected."

She sat down next to him. Near their feet, a red Oregon rock crab scurried across the sand, then disappeared beneath a granite slab. Farther beyond, a group of sandpipers peeped as they ran along the shore, stopping and starting like a tiny black and white chorus line.

"It's so great to see the healthy seabirds and a much, much cleaner beach," Joanna said, breaking into a wide smile. "When I called Trudy to check on the final tally, she said nearly twenty-five tons of plastic were collected during the cleanup."

"Ted and I were just talking about the other day when I stopped in at Anchorhold to chat. He expects over time to see a difference in the number of animals brought in there."

"I'm not surprised. The cleanup was one of the most successful on record. Workers on a beach north of here even found two car hoods, a couple of refrigerators, and five televisions."

"Wow!" Austin chuckled. "I'd hate to have been the poor soul who hauled all that stuff in."

Nodding, she chuckled too.

They talked on and on, taking in the tranquil seascape, the hidden wonders in each other's eyes. Sometimes they spoke solemnly. Other times they laughed.

And when Austin had finally gathered her into his arms, his lips urgently seeking hers, Joanna knew she'd come one foolish step closer to falling in love.

Chapter Eight

"Thank goodness for Auntie," Joanna said to herself the next morning as she backed the car onto the main road. An early riser, a woman filled with quiet wisdom and strong conviction, Marcella was always at her kitchen table by five-thirty every morning to read and meditate. If anyone could help Joanna sort through her turmoil, it'd surely be Auntie. Truth was, she'd outlived two husbands.

"What a surprise!" Marcella exclaimed when she greeted Joanna at her front door a short time later. "And what a relief to see you back on your feet."

"Oh, Auntie!" Joanna enveloped the older woman in a gentle hug. She felt so small and frail, Joanna marveled she hadn't fractured any bones that day she fell. "I'm sorry I couldn't help when you needed me."

"Nonsense, child." They drew back, surveying each other at arm's length. "All I did was get a little bump on my head," Marcella continued. "I'm still not sure why Austin insisted on rushing me to the hospital—though he was such a dear."

At the sound of Austin's name, Joanna's stomach twisted. "But *I'm* here now. I'm here for whatever you might need me to do."

The familiar, old-fashioned kitchen, with its sheer Priscilla curtains, Formica countertops, and red-and-white canisters, gave her a fleeting modicum of comfort. So much the way she remembered it as a child when she and her family used to visit. Even the smells were the same—the faint rose scent of hand soap mingled with lemony floor wax.

"All I need now is the pleasure of your company," the older woman said, running a gnarled hand through silvery, permed hair. She motioned to a kitchen table chair, and Joanna sank gratefully into it. "My freezer is chock-full. I have at least a three month's supply of medicine. And there's a lady coming once a week to help with the cleaning until Lucille gets back—she's the wife of another doctor in town, a charming woman by the name of Helen. Austin made sure he left no stones unturned."

"Hmm. Most likely Ted Ashelman's wife," Joanna murmured, more to herself than Aunt Marcella. Though Austin had obviously forgotten to tell her about that, she knew he was quickly becoming good friends with both Ted and Helen.

Joanna looked away, trying to hide the pain she was certain reflected in her face. Truth was, the rest of the day after her and Austin's romantic interlude on the beach, they'd spoken very little. The tension had been like an ominous wall casting its looming shadow between them.

Is everything all right, dear?" Aunt Marcella couldn't be fooled as she narrowed her gray eyes on Joanna.

"Yes. No. Oh, Auntie, I'm really not sure."

Pulling up a chair next to Joanna and sitting down, Marcella covered her niece's hand with her own. Tortuous blue veins flattened beneath transparent skin as she gave an encouraging squeeze. "So what is it?" she asked. "Not your new job, I hope."

"Oh no! The job's fine. It's everything I've wanted for a long, long time. I'm looking forward to going back tomorrow." Joanna glanced down at her aunt's wire-framed reading glasses, a bottle of aspirin, and the old white leather Bible on the kitchen table.

"Good. I'm glad to hear you say that."

"My problem's Austin," Joanna said in a rush before Marcella could ask more.

"Ah, yes." A faint smiled lifted the older woman's lips. "The very likeness of Kyle himself."

"Oh, that's just it! Kyle *and Austin*. Fighting back tears, she poured out her heart, struggled to describe her escalating confusion. "Sometimes I feel so guilty . . . spending time with Austin, enjoying myself, letting him help me."

"He's not only a sight for sore eyes, he's also one of the most thoughtful young men I've ever known," Marcella agreed.

"Yes . . . yes. He's *too* handsome, *too* thoughtful. I . . . I never thought I'd enjoy the company of another man, experience such completeness with anyone other than Kyle." She gulped before going on. "This is Kyle's brother we're talking about, Auntie. His *only* brother. I mean, what would Kyle say?"

"He'd say you're young and beautiful. That he wants you to let go of your grief and live out a full, happy life. And if it turns out that his own flesh and blood is the one to show you how, then so much the better."

"But I feel like I'm a traitor, dishonoring our marriage." The older woman's face suddenly wavered through a new surge of tears. "And . . . and this isn't fair to Austin either. Even if I did let myself love him, I could never love him truly for himself. I'm afraid Austin would always be a substitute for Kyle."

Marcella tapped her chin thoughtfully with one finger, pursed her lips, then said, "Time, my dear. Healing takes time, but the healing *will* come. When your Uncle Benjamin died, I thought I'd never again see the light of day. But then a few years later, I met Marcus. True, there weren't any family ties, but I still experienced my share of guilt, spent many a night of soul-searching. In the end, I came to realize that while no one could ever take Ben's place, I could love Marcus in a whole new way." She steepled her hands together, peering at Joanna directly over them. "Some day you'll come to that place in your life too, dear. And when the time is right, no one—not even me—will need to tell you."

***

Joanna maneuvered the Subaru back into the driveway and spotted Austin, Ted Ashelman, and Grant Conner, crouched atop the duplex roof, stripping it down to the tar paper. The sun shone through a mellow haze, and the temperature hovered around a pleasant sixty degrees. "Perfect roofing weather," Austin had said that morning.

They continued working all day till early evening, while Joanna kept a steady supply of submarine sandwiches and iced tea coming.

Later, as Ted had promised, they all drove back to the Ashelmans' for an old-fashioned clambake—complete with parsleyed potatoes, crispy coleslaw, and a fresh apple pie. Trudy was already there, helping Ted's wife peel the apples. It wasn't long before Joanna, too, had fetched a paring knife and was sitting at the kitchen table, chatting and laughing with the other two women.

After the picnic table was cleared, the three couples donned lightweight jackets to linger beneath the soft glow of the backyard lights while an amber harvest moon inched higher. Despite the men's good-humored complaints about sore knees and aching backs, they all agreed it had been a satisfying day.

The following week, the roof was finally completed. Meanwhile, Austin had been so occupied with a myriad of finishing details, and Joanna so busy catching up on her work at the aquarium, their spare time together was sorely limited.

Yet every evening when she returned home and walked through the front door, her heart soared at the sight of him. Now Joanna's longing grew deeper, creating a vacuum she knew only Austin could fill. *Is this the meaning behind Marcella's words?* Joanna asked herself. Was it time to let go of the shackles that had bound her?

Yes! her heart cried. The answer was unequivocally yes. Though she would never, ever stop loving Kyle, she was at last free to love Austin wholly, without reservation. She loved him because he was Austin Sullivan, a man in his own right, a gentle giant who had captured her very heart and soul.

But any day now, he'd be gone. The work was done, and there was no way she could expect him to stay longer. All for the best, her better judgment insisted. Though she hadn't missed Austin's fleeting, tender glances, nor failed to luxuriate in his fiery kisses, she also hadn't mistaken the tension that kept building with each passing day. Did she dare dream that somehow he loved her too?

***

"Where were you?" Stacey asked plaintively on the other end of the phone. "I thought you had Friday afternoons off. I've been calling forever!"

"I've been at Anchorhold."

"Oh, yeah! Now I remember. That wild animal clinic." A brief silence followed. "So what do you do there?" Stacey asked.

"Feed and water the animals, clean cages. Today Ted even let me assist him with surgery. Someone brought in a fawn with a broken leg."

"Not my idea of fun!" Stacey returned with a giggle. "Any time I get a break from classes, I always head for the mall."

Joanna laughed too. "And that could prove a disaster for a poor, starving college student like you. So what's up, kiddo?" She looked back over her shoulder at Austin, who'd wandered into the front room where she was talking.

"I met a brand-new guy by the name of Robert. He's so cool!"

"What happened to the other two guys?"

"I ditched them when I met Robert. Honest, this time it's for real. I never knew what love was all about till now."

"I'm glad, Stace. That's terrific." Though Joanna's reply was sincere, she couldn't help smiling at Stacey's capricious manner. Joanna's own college days seemed an eternity ago.

"I have two weeks off at Christmastime," Stacey babbled on, "and Robert said he might be able to fly out with me. I can hardly wait for you to meet him." She paused. "That'll be okay, won't it? Okay for Robert to come too?"

"Why . . . er, of course."

"Good. Because we've already got our plane tickets. Everything's arranged."

Joanna stole another glance at Austin, who was standing with his back turned to her, his stance rigid as he stared out the window. Something was wrong. "Look, Stace, we'll talk about this more again soon, but I've got to scoot. I'll call you back soon, okay?"

"Oh! All right. Promise you won't forget?'

"I promise. Later."

"Yeah, later."

"That was Stace," Joanna said, tucking her phone into her pocket. Momentarily forgetting her uneasiness, she shook her head as she turned to look at Austin. "Sometimes I think her life is nothing but one big soap opera. It's hard to remember a time I felt that way—if I ever did."

"Stacey's doing well in school?"

"Yes." She shifted beneath his steady gaze.

"Good." He hesitated. "Jo, we need to talk. Right now."

"Uh . . . sure." Her knees felt weak. *This is it. He's going to tell me it's time for him to go. From now on, it'll be just like before. An occasional brief phone call. A greeting card at Christmas. Yes, the same as before, but a thousand times different.* At the thought, a deep ache filled her.

"I hope I didn't appear rude," he said, avoiding her eyes. "I didn't mean for it to seem as if I was eavesdropping on your conversation with Stacey. It's just . . . well, I knew if I didn't get right on with it, I might lose my nerve."

A knot rose in her chest, making her feel as if she couldn't get enough air. "What is it?"

"We need to talk about Kyle."

"Yes."

He started pacing, his hands linked behind his back. "The day I arrived here," his words tumbled over themselves, "I told you about how he always wanted to be a firefighter, how he rebelled against our parents' wishes, and how I supported him."

"And?"

"I didn't tell you the entire story." He stopped pacing and faced her squarely. "There's a lot more." His gaze flicked momentarily away. "You may remember my saying how I blamed myself that Kyle lost his life. Well, I think I've finally come to terms with that, just like I'm pretty sure you've come to better terms with your own grieving." He faltered before going on. "I realize now—thanks to some terrific talks I've had with Ted—that regardless of anything I may have told him, the choice was ultimately Kyle's."

"Of course it was." She swallowed hard. "Besides, he died doing what he loved the most."

"But he also died knowing he was leaving you behind." Austin's face darkened. "Shortly before he asked you to marry him," he continued, "Kyle came to me to ask a favor. My brother knew he'd chosen a high-risk profession and was concerned about your welfare if something should ever happen to him."

She nodded. "Yes. We talked about that—but only a little."

"Still, what you didn't talk about, I know, was my promise to him."

"What promise?" Apprehension, like spiked icicles, stabbed at her as she read the anguish mirrored on his handsome face.

"Kyle asked me to swear that I'd look out for you till you were back on your feet. Of course, at the time, I'm sure that neither of us believed that would ever really come about. A little denial can sometimes help take the rough edge off things, you know."

"So that's why you decided to stick around and help me?" she asked in a small voice.

"Yes. I have to confess," Austin continued, "in the beginning, I did a pretty half-baked job of making good my promise. Every time I called, it sounded as if you had it all together. I figured you'd made the adjustment as well as could be expected, that there was no need for me to keep closer tabs on you." He paused, studying her intently. "But when I arrived here in Southport, thinking I was only passing through town, I realized I made a humongous mistake."

She forced her eyes from his. She felt a numbing sensation as the truth seeped in. So Austin's concern had been driven by mere duty. And now he was still duty-bound. The yellow roses, the intimate dinners, the romantic walks on the beach . . . they'd all meant nothing.

"But why didn't Kyle tell me this?" she asked.

"Kyle realize from practically the first day he met you that you were independent and proud. He believed if he explained about our agreement, you would insist it wasn't necessary. That's why I've held out till now too. I was afraid if you sent me away, I'd have lived the rest of my life wrestling with an even greater guilt—the guilt of knowing I shirked my responsibility."

"So ultimately Kyle didn't think I could make it on my own?"

"No, it wasn't that exactly. He just loved you so much, Jo. He didn't want to see you struggle unnecessarily." His eyes locked with hers. "But now it appears you've gotten through it. You have a terrific job, new friends too. You've dedicated yourself to the things that mean so much to you." He spread his hands. "And the work here is done. You can advertise for tenants any time now."

"Yes." She stood up too, hugging her arms about her chest. Tears burned at the back of her throat. If life was so wonderful, why was this foreboding dark cloud pressing down on her?

"As you know, I didn't bring much," he went on. "It won't take me long to pack."

She inhaled a steadying breath. "When do you plan to leave?"

"First thing in the morning. But this is it for us, Jo. I'm saying good-bye right now."

***

Austin peered through the light rain at the ribbon of highway that snaked ahead. It was a few minutes past five. Off to a great start, he thought. The best time of day to be hitting the road.

As he sped on, he caught sight of an occasional light glittering through a house window. Early risers. Families. Perhaps husbands and wives, sitting down together over morning coffee. Or parents feeding little ones in high chairs, preparing for another busy day.

Vroom, vroom. He could still remember those childhood scenes . . . a bit hazy, perhaps, but still fixed in his mind. He remembered how his parents had played airplane with Kyle whenever they attempted to feed him hot cooked cereal or pureed prunes. How, sometimes, he'd taken his turn at helping feed Kyle too. Though his parents had been away a lot pursuing their professions, they were nevertheless a happy family. At the thought, his gut twisted. His eyes smarted.

"Better get on with it, man," he murmured aloud. "This is what you've been wanting, isn't it? To finally break free? To be on your way again, heading for that fishing lodge?"

Then why am I feeling so totally down? he wondered. As if a crucial part of him, from somewhere deep inside, had been ripped out and thrown away forever?

He kept driving, past towering evergreens, small beach towns, and idyllic scenes with old-fashioned farmhouses, the kind one sometimes saw on Christmas cards.

Yes, Christmas, he mused, chewing on his lower lip. Already it was less than two months away. Did he really want to spend another one back in San Francisco, hobnobbing with the big boys at parties and fund-raisers, toasting in the holidays and wearing a phony smile, then trudging back alone to his empty condo?

No. He didn't.

The void inside of him expanded like a heavy weight pressing in all directions from inside his chest. At first when he'd opted for his three month leave, he figured all it would take to get his head on straight was a fishing trip in the wilds. But something had happened these past four weeks. Something that left him restless and unfulfilled.

It was getting a little lighter now. To the west, a finger of land jutted out. At the end, he could make out the faint form of a lighthouse with its pulsating beacon. Back on the highway, the traffic was growing heavier. More travelers. Folks on their way to offices, schools, and medical facilities.

In his mind, he mapped out the trip ahead. He'd keep heading up the coast highway till he could pick up a major route that veered east. Then he would hook into the interstate and continue north into Washington.

Maybe he'd hole up for the night in Seattle. Or somewhere this side of the Canadian border. Maybe he'd even look up that old girlfriend in Bellingham . . . let's see, wasn't Audrey her name?

At any rate, the Jeep seemed to be driving a bit ragged. During his first stop to gas up, he'd have to check it out.

Gripping the steering wheel harder, he willed himself to smile. Yep, he was finally on his way again. But were his troubles really over?

Chapter Nine

Joanna arose after a fitful night's sleep and peered outside the front room window at the driveway. Fresh sorrow filled her as she stared at the empty spot where Austin had always parked his Jeep.

There was no mistake. He was truly gone. An hour earlier, at the dawn's first light, while she lay awake staring unseeingly at the shadows on the bedroom wall, she heard the rev of his motor, and then the crunch of gravel as he'd backed onto the road.

Heaving a sigh, she stared at the lawn and noticed a light dusting of frost. The sky, the color of pewter, was growing brighter. The early morning chill seemed to underscore the emptiness filling her. *How can I ever go on without him?* she asked herself as she rummaged through her closet in search of something to wear. She'd have to—somehow. She'd survived sorrow before, she could do it again.

Yet the hurt slashed deeply, to her very core. Duty. Honor. Such noble ideals. What good were they in the absence of love?

Still, isn't that just like Austin? she reasoned, remembering the story he had shared about Kyle and his youth. Austin had been the dependable son. The one who'd honored their parents' wishes. Why should it be any different now?

Perhaps that was partly why she'd been attracted to Austin in the first place, and why now she cared for him deeply. He had appeared in her life—like a fortress, a rock—when she'd been frightened and vulnerable.

And though she couldn't deny what he'd said about her pride, she needed him now—not because he was someone she could lean on, but because she'd grown to love and respect him. She yearned to share every part of her life with him for the rest of her days.

Would she ever hear from him again? Would it be the same as before? No, it could never be the same, she knew in an instant. Her love for him had changed everything. Her hopes. Her dreams. The way she felt when she looked at him, touched him.

The rest of the day at the aquarium, she kept busy with unnecessary details, attempting to fill every spare moment to blot out any thoughts of Austin. Yes, life still could have meaning, she kept reassuring herself. She mustn't allow herself to lose sight of that again. She simply must not.

Truth was she had a job she loved, a home near the beach, and Friday afternoons at Anchorhold. What more did she need?

Yet try as she did to forget about Austin, pictures of him kept floating up in her mind. Where was he right now? Was he still traveling the Interstate? Was he standing on the deck of some ferry, the wind whipping through his dark hair? Was his handsome, tanned face etched against a backdrop of blue?

"Joanna, what's wrong?" Trudy asked after they'd locked the front doors at closing time and wandered inside Trudy's office to talk.

"Nothing. I'm . . . just a little preoccupied, that's all," she lied. She sank down into the large swivel chair that faced the massive desk, while Trudy seated herself across from her.

"Come on, fess up." Trudy reached out and touched her hand. "I might be your boss, but I'm a friend now too. Hopefully a good friend."

"Oh, Trudy, of course, you're a good friend. And I'm thankful for that . . ." Her voice trailed off. She shut her eyes momentarily, as if somehow doing so would blot out the pain.

"It's Austin. Am I right? she heard Trudy murmur.

"I . . . I'm afraid so." Joanna opened her eyes and stared down at her lap, twisting the strap of her handbag. "He's gone, Trudy."

"When did he leave?"

"This morning. Early." Haltingly, Joanna told her what Austin had said the night before. "I love him. I love him so much, but . . . but it's obvious he'll never feel the same way about me. I doubt if I'll ever see him again."

"You're wrong," Trudy insisted. "He'll be back. You wait. I'm willing to bet my life on it."

"What makes you so sure?"

Trudy sent her a knowing smile. "Don't think I missed the way he was looking at you the other night at Ted and Helen's."

"At one time I might've agreed with you, but now I know better." She shook her head. "Austin was just happy. Happy the roof was done. Happy he would finally be on his way."

"I don't think so. A man who is just happy wouldn't have that certain look on his face, like any minute he was ready to take you into his arms and kiss the everlasting daylights out of you."

Joanna shook her head, blinking back tears. "Thanks for the encouragement, Trudy, but when it comes to love, I don't need false hope."

"It's not false hope. I'm never wrong."

Joanna had to bite her lip to keep from pointing out that this time she just might be.

After all, there was always a first time for everything.

***

A telephone ringing threaded through Joanna's dream, and in an instant she realized it wasn't a dream. It was the familiar ringtone from her phone. Fumbling, squinting against the early morning light, she finally managed to answer it. Who was calling so early? Was something wrong? She held a hand to her heart. *Please don't let it be about Austin. Please not a car wreck . . .*

"Joanna! It's Ted."

"Ted?" She gave an audible sigh of relief. "Oh, thank heavens!"

"Are you awake?"

The urgency in his voice cleared her last traces of drowsiness. "What's the matter?"

"We got a problem! About an hour ago, the Fish and Wildlife Services phoned. There's been a small oil spill off the shores of Southport."

"What happened? When?" She sat bolt upright now, gripping the phone so tightly her hands throbbed. She peered over at her nightstand. The digital clock next to the lamp said five forty-five.

"I don't have all the details yet, but they said a tanker struck a reef. Happened a couple hours ago, I think. There's going to be an early-morning news alert on television in less than fifteen minutes, but I doubt if many folks are up yet to hear it."

A slow, sickening sensation gripped her. How could this be? Was this some crazy nightmare? A cruel twist of fate? The beach cleanup had proved a hug success.

And now this . . .

"Too many seabirds have already perished, others have managed to reach land, but they're struggling for survival," the veterinarian continued, slicing through her spiraling thoughts.

"How bad is it, Ted? How many birds?" Her heart hammered with fresh fear.

"It's too early to know for sure, of course. I've heard the count so far has just topped four thousand. Puffins, murres, scoters, to name a few. The seals, otters, fish, and bivalves are at risk also, but right now we must concentrate on the seabirds."

"So where should we start? What should we do first?"

"I'm heading over to Anchorhold as soon as I can, but first I'm gonna have to drive into town to round up some supplies. Luckily, we have those empty portables out back, so we can set up a temporary treatment center there."

"Will one center be enough? Especially if the birds continue to pour in?"

"I doubt it. I've made arrangements for another center at the old grange hall off 101. We're gonna need more vets, too. Hopefully my interns can hold down the fort at the grange while I do what I can at Anchorhold."

For a painful instant, her thoughts skirted to Austin, but Ted's voice reigned her in again.

"Can you drive straightaway to Anchorhold, Joanna? Get things organized till I can get there too?"

"Of course!"

"Good. I'll need you to round up as many volunteers as possible. Meanwhile, we'll have to set up triage stations and feeding and bathing areas."

"I'll call Trudy right away. I'm sure she'll give me as much time off as necessary."

"Swell. I also plan to see whether we can use the Boy Scout camp, should it turn out we need a backup."

After they exchanged hasty good-byes and Joanna phoned Trudy, she shrugged into a sweatshirt, then pulled on a pair of jeans.

Her head reeled with the necessary preparations. Volunteers. They'd need a ton of them, not only to rescue the birds off the beaches, but for the critical follow-up care. Where had Austin placed the list of those who'd turned out for the beach cleanup? she wondered. Could they also round up enough heat lamps, syringes, stomach tubes, and washtubs, tables for drying, recovery pens, and flotation test tanks?

Though Joanna's degree in environmental studies had prepared her for such a crisis—academically speaking—she'd never faced a real oil spill. Right now the task seemed daunting.

***

Austin grabbed a cup of espresso and a cinnamon roll at the hotel coffee shop, then checked out at the registration desk. He'd stopped for the night on the outskirts of Seattle and now, early morning again, he was eager to be on his way.

Outside, his Jeep windshield was covered with frost. He noted a nip in the air. Yep, Old Man Winter would soon be on his way, he reminded himself. And there were only four more weeks till his leave would run out. Better pack in all the fishing he could. Soon it would be time to drive back to California.

He turned the key in the ignition and let the engine idle, while he rummaged through his glove compartment for an ice scraper. A few minutes later, the windows cleared, he climbed back into the driver's seat and rubbed his hands together, then shoved the heater on full blast.

"On the road again," he crooned, admittedly a little off-key. Yet somehow it just didn't feel right. Is this really what he wanted to do?

He shifted into drive. With a high-pitched whine, the Jeep barely crept across the parking lot. Then it stopped cold.

"Damn! What's going on?" he exclaimed, his frustration mushrooming.

Later, after the tow truck had arrived, Austin sat in the customer waiting area of the nearest garage, his head in his hands. Several other customers waited also. Obviously it was going to take a while before he learned what was wrong.

A mechanic finally emerged through the door. "I'm afraid, sir, your transmission is shot."

"But are you sure? The guy at the gas station said my fluid was low, so I had him—"

"I'm sorry, sir. Maybe it was low then, but it looks as if that was only part of your problem."

"Great!" Austin said, rubbing the back of his neck with one hand.

"We're running behind now, but we'll try to get the work done as soon as we can. Probably in a day or two."

As Austin gave the go-ahead for the repairs, his hopes dwindled. Would he ever make it to Canada?

Luckily, the hotel where he'd stayed last night was within walking distance of the garage. He'd go back and pay for another night. At least the beds were pretty decent, he consoled himself. And the high definition television in his room sure beat that pathetic little set Joanna had loaned him.

Back inside the same room again—no one had reserved it—he sank into the love seat and flipped on the early morning news.

"And now for the local events," the announcer was saying in a monotone. "We've just received a bulletin from the Coast Guard and Oregon State Fish and Wildlife Services. Authorities have reported that during the early morning hours, a tanker struck a reef about fifty miles off the coast of Southport, resulting in a two-hundred-thousand-gallon oil spill."

Austin's jaw dropped. He sprang to his feet, his gaze fixed on the TV screen.

"Meanwhile, thousands of birds and marine wildlife are at risk," the announcer continued. "Volunteers from all over the Pacific Northwest are flooding the beaches, trying to organize rescue efforts. Please stay tuned for further details."

"Oh, no!" he groaned. Where was Joanna right now? Had she gotten involved? *Stupid question,* he answered himself with a swift mental kick. Of course she had! Ted too!

He gritted his teeth. His thoughts spun. He had no choice but to go back. He must call the garage immediately. Insist that they push the work through.

Ted needed him—and so did Jo.

***

Joanna worked tirelessly, not even stopping to snatch a few hours' sleep. Twenty-four long hours had dragged on since she'd received the call from Ted. While the interns supervised the rescue efforts at the other two treatment centers, she and Ted headed up the work at Anchorhold.

Word about the oil spill had spread quickly, and throngs of volunteers had met the challenge.

Irrepressible sadness filled Joanna at the sight of so many birds fighting for their lives, yet at the same time she felt unexpectedly encouraged. In less than two days, more folks had turned out than she had ever imagined. High school and college students, senior citizens, young families—the list went on and on.

Meanwhile, seabirds, both living and dead, were carried from the shorelines to waiting trucks and vans, then transported to the nearest treatment center. Some flapped with fright, others were weak and lethargic, on the brink of death.

The oil, roughly half an inch thick, had matted their feathers and soaked through to their skin, destroying their natural insulation and buoyancy. After triaging and tagging, the birds were warmed, tube-fed an electrolyte solution, and placed in pens. Later, after ample time to adjust to their new surroundings, they were given warm baths in a one percent detergent solution.

Joanna's shoulders sagged with fatigue as she and a sandy-haired teenage named Derek bathed perhaps the hundredth bird they'd admitted several hours earlier that day.

While Derek held the disgruntled murre with gloved hands in a dishpan of soapy water, Joanna scrubbed meticulously, covering every inch of the bird's body. So far it had taken nearly half an hour to unmat each layer of oil-soaked feathers, and by the time they were done, it'd most likely be double that time. Dental picks and cotton swabs proved handy for the especially tough spots.

The murre craned its neck and thrashed, shrieking whenever Joanna momentarily lost her hold on its pointed, dark bill. Everywhere about them came similar squawks, the steady murmur of the workers' voices, the loud beating of wings.

"There, there," Joanna crooned, while Derek helped her turn the bird onto its back to have its belly bathed next. "Once we're done here and you're nice and dry in a warm, clean pen, you'll thank me for this." She wrinkled her nose, still unaccustomed to the musky smell of wet feathers mingled with the more pungent odor of the crude oil.

"Nice and dry—sounds good to me," Derek commented with a chuckle. He stared down at his own water-soaked jeans and laughed again. "My Mom's gonna kill me if I catch a cold." Though the community volunteers had donned make-shift aprons from plastic garbage bags, most hadn't escaped the bursts of water caused by the struggling birds.

"When is your shift over, Derek?" Joanna asked, stifling a yawn. She looked down, suddenly aware that her own coveralls and boots were covered with the sudsy water also.

"I'm supposed to leave in about fifteen minutes or so," Derek Answered. "Someone from my biology class is coming to relieve me. We're getting extra credit for this." He tightened his grasp on the murre and added eagerly, "but I don't mind if I have to stick around longer. Helping here is really cool. Besides," he added, "it was kind of fun staying up all night."

Joanna nodded. "And as for me, I never dreamed so many people would turn out. It's wonderful."

"So when do we get to see whether the birds can float again?" Derek asked.

"Not for awhile. They'll need to stay in their clean pens till they've had a chance to get over their trauma. If the birds have suffered injuries, like cuts or bruises, they'll need time to heal physically also." She smiled at the boy's apparent eagerness and added, "And after the birds are tested in the float pools, many will need to be rewashed, dried, and tested again. This is perhaps the most crucial—"

The sound of a deep, flawlessly modulated masculine voice coming from somewhere near the triage station stopped her next words.

She tossed a look over her shoulder.

Austin!

Shock waves washed over her. She felt the color drain from her face. When had he arrived? How long had he been standing next to Ted, helping him assess the birds' medical needs? She'd been so engrossed in what she was doing, she'd never even noticed.

For a split second, Austin looked up, met her eyes, and smiled.

She had to look away. Her pulse was racing much too fast. Her hands trembled as she refocused her attention on the struggling murre and started to scrub a little faster.

"You feeling okay, Ms. Sullivan?" Derek's voice penetrated her shock and confusion. "You don't look so good."

"I . . . I'm just tired. I guess . . . guess maybe I need some sleep."

"Yeah, we all do."

Why had Austin returned, she wondered, then decided he'd most likely heard about the oil spill on his Jeep radio and driven immediately back. But most of all, why had he come *here*? Why couldn't he have chosen one of the other treatment centers instead? Goodness only knew, all three were desperate for skilled veterinarians. It was going to be next to impossible—no *utterly* impossible having to keep her composure with Austin Sullivan sticking so close by.

A short time later, after the murre was thoroughly rinsed and dried, Joanna wandered into the employees' lounge, where ladies from the community were serving hot beverages, fruit punch, and doughnuts.

She needed to get away for a moment. Away where she wouldn't have to hear Austin's voice, where she wouldn't have to fight the temptation to steal just one more look at him.

Joanna helped herself to a cup of strong coffee and sipped it gratefully. Though volunteers filtered in and out, drinking from paper cups and chatting as if attending a church social, the tension beneath their smiles was all too apparent. More seabirds were arriving with each passing hour.

"I fed your cat."

Joanna lifted her gaze. Austin was standing only inches away.

"What?"

"I said I fed your cat. I stopped by the duplex first . . . and noticed yesterday's and this morning's *Sea-scroll* on our . . .uh . . . your front porch, so I thought I'd better go inside to check on Silky."

"Thanks," she said tightly. She suddenly remembered he'd never returned his key. "But rest assured, I didn't forget my personal obligations," she went on. "The next-door neighbor agreed to make sure Silky had plenty of food and fresh water in case I couldn't get home often enough to take care of that. And Lucille's back now to look in on Aunt Marcella."

He hesitated, then said gruffly, "I wasn't inferring you were ignoring your responsibilities. But right now I think you'd better go home and hit the sack. I bet you've been up all night. You look exhausted."

"You don't look so hot yourself."

"I suppose not. I drove straight through." He lowered his voice. "I'll explain everything to Ted. Tell him it was my idea you take off."

"I can't go home. There's too much work to do."

His gaze was steady, unwavering. "It's not good, Jo, you pushing yourself this way."

She struggled to keep her temper at bay. Who was he to show up like this again, totally unannounced, then tell her how to run her life? His responsibility for her was done. Over.

"Tell me something," she said, changing the subject. "Exactly why did you come back? Was it your underlying sense of duty, Austin?"

He flinched, then wrenched his eyes from hers. "Isn't that what you wanted? For me to get involved with the rescue efforts too?"

"Of course. But that depends on the reason behind it. In other words, don't do me any favors." She folded her arms across her chest, silently challenging him to look at her again.

He did.

"I came because I knew I was needed. It's that simple."

"Ah, so like you. But is that the sum of your well-ordered life? Austin Sullivan, the good guy. Everyone's hero." The spite she heard in her voice surprised her. Maybe she was more exhausted than she realized. Or maybe she loved him far too much. More than she could ever admit to herself—or him.

"And getting back to your pointing out what's good for me," she hurried on, giving full vent to her anger, "there's no need! You've fulfilled your promise to your little brother. His merry widow is finally safe and secure. From now on, you can jolly well wipe her from your mind and conscience."

His eyes suddenly sparked with . . . with what? Anger? Confusion? Regret? Certainly not love.

"Look," he ground out. "We need to get this settled." He glanced first left, then right. "Let's go outside." He yanked at the top button of his shirt collar, and it popped off. "Besides, it's getting too blasted hot."

"If you intend to rope me into another one of your talks, forget it. How can you deny it?" He squared his jaw, then impaled her with his magnetic gaze. "Come on. My Jeep's in the parking lot." Clasping her hand in his, he led the way.

A rush of cool air assaulted her as they hurried outside.

"This is ridiculous!" she protested. He swung open the passenger door and waited while she climbed inside. "We said good-bye two nights ago."

"I think we have more to say than simply good-bye." He slammed the Jeep door, then stalked around to his side and slid in.

"Like what?"

"Like what's eating you? Why are you angry with me? I was only doing what Kyle asked. Wouldn't you do the same for *your* little sister?"

She couldn't bear to look at him. Tears of humiliation and hurt were flowing too fast. How could she face him and admit she'd fallen in love with him? It was impossible—and foolhardy.

"Of course, I'd help Stacey," she said between sobs. "But that's different. A whole lot different." Getting a hold of herself, she continued in a torrent of breathless words. "I'm not sure exactly what you plan to do now or how long you intend to stay. But I think it'd be best if we don't see each other—except, of course, for the unavoidable times here."

"You don't know what you're saying. You're exhausted. Wiped out. You'll regret this later, believe me."

"No, I won't."

"Joanna." The edge in his voice had softened. "Please! Please don't do this." He lifted her chin in one palm, his eyes imploring. Softly he grazed her cheek with his other hand, then wiped away the moisture. Pressing her hand to his lips, he held it there for an immeasurable moment.

New tears fell, bittersweet, splashing onto his hand.

"Let me go!" She pulled away, then shoved open the Jeep door and dashed back inside Anchorhold.

She couldn't allow him to keep playing with her heart this way. It was already shattered into too many pieces.

Chapter Ten

"Damn!" Austin slammed a fist against the steering wheel as he listened to Joanna's footsteps fade away. What was it about this woman that made her so right, so totally irresistible?

After what had just happened, he should be furious, feeling put down.

But he wasn't. And he doubted if he ever could feel that way. No . . . not about Joanna.

These past four weeks with her had been a whole lot of heaven and a little bit of hell. It was downright scary, the way she was getting to him—and now it was worse than ever. But why? It didn't make sense. Had he been kidding himself when he said the only reason he'd come back was because of the oil spill?

He stared uncomprehendingly into the early morning light. She certainly wasn't the first female he'd enjoyed kissing, holding in his arms, spending time with. But she just could be the last.

Wait—that was ludicrous! What was coming over him? Permanent commitments were sticky business. Something he'd always made certain to avoid. Besides, there was no way they could ever patch things up. She was too wounded. Perhaps even feeling betrayed. But why? Why did his motives matter to her so? Could she have fallen in love with him?

Did he love her?

A Suburban turned into the lot and parked a few spaces down as his thoughts churned on. Whatever was beneath all this, he'd better get control of himself. Fast. This wasn't like him, allowing his emotions to turn to mush—especially over a woman.

Kyle's woman.

Raking a hand through his hair, he climbed out of the Jeep and gave the door a hard slam. Time to get back to work, he told himself, peering again at the Suburban, where workers were unloading several dozen more birds.

Yes, that was the answer. He'd have to keep busy. Throw himself back into the rescue efforts. And by the looks of things, he quickly decided, that wouldn't be too difficult.

***

Three weeks passed, and the birds continued to pour in, till finally by the fourth week, the numbers had begun to dwindle.

"Unfortunately, only time will tell the full outcome of the spill on the birds' total populations," Joanna explained to a new group of students who had turned out to help at Anchorhold. "Seabirds that came in contact with just small amounts of oil may still succumb after they've preened and digested it. Breeding patterns may be seriously altered also. But I've been amazed at the fortitude of those that have survived."

Wide-eyed, their gazes fixed on Joanna, they'd crowded in closer and nodded their agreement.

There'd been so much work at Anchorhold to occupy Joanna's energy and time, she'd somehow managed to get through in spite of Austin. Yet as her spirits sank lower with each passing day, her hurt and confusion remained open and raw.

During this interim, she saw little of Austin. He rotated shifts among all three treatment centers and always slept over at Ted and Helen's. Still, she couldn't escape those occasions when their paths *did* cross— eyes meeting eyes in a highly charged current of unspoken tension.

Funny thing, she found herself thinking during her more rare moments of quiet reflection. *Strange how life sometimes turns out*—in this case, one might even call it a paradox.

In the beginning, when Austin first arrived, she'd yearned for this—yearned for him to share her passion for preserving the Earth, the wildlife, the beaches. What good now were common interests and goals when a future between them could never be?

Yet despite her unhappiness, Joanna was deeply touched at the tremendous outpouring of caring and love from so many people. There'd been those who had combed the beaches with painstaking deliberateness, the volunteers who had labored long hours at the treatment centers, plus the community members who'd continued to provide warm food and words of encouragement. Good-hearted people had come from both near and far.

"It's incredible," Joanna said to Trudy during a brief phone call to bring her up to date. "Though we've managed to save and release less than half of the birds brought in, it gives me so much hope to see the way the people have rallied."

"That's right," Trudy agreed. "I'm hearing similar comments here at the aquarium. It might be a cliché about the silver lining around each dark cloud," she went on, "but I think that's the best way of summing this all up. Though the oil spill was certainly a catastrophe, the human response to it made all the difference."

"Exactly." Joanna's voice caught. "I couldn't have said it better myself." Unexpectedly, her thoughts rolled back to Austin. She couldn't help wondering whether Trudy had heard about his return and especially what had happened between them.

Did Trudy still believe *their* dark cloud was lined in silver?

***

"So what's it gonna be, pal?" Ted Ashelman asked Austin, giving him a long, hard look. "Made up your mind yet?"

"About what?" Austin asked evasively.

"You know. You gonna take me up on my offer? Sign on as my partner here at Anchorhold?"

The two veterinarians were loading up a pickup with gray and white horned grebes. All morning long, they'd been hard at work as they'd prepared for the release of the remaining birds.

"I haven't made up my mind yet, Ted. It's a tough call."

"Listen. Life's full of tough decisions. And you're gonna have to quit dillydallying. Didn't you say you're due back at the zoo in three short days?"

Austin latched the door closed on a plywood-sided pen, hefted it into the pickup, all the while avoiding the older man's eyes. "Yes. Three more days," he answered. "This means I should probably be taking off tomorrow."

"And that's what you want?"

"I . . . I already told you, Ashelman. I still don't know."

Ted hitched himself on to the tailgate of the pickup and looked directly at Austin. "So what's it gonna take to bring you to your senses? A swift kick in your indecisive rear? I think you do know. You just don't want to face it, pal. The real problem is you and your little lady, isn't it?"

Austin swallowed hard as he took three steps back. His voice hardened. "Joanna's not mine! She's my brother's wife."

"Your brother's dead, Austin. Dead and buried. You're not."

"We've already been over that," Austin snapped. "You—of all people—should know I'm finally getting it together again."

"True, but you haven't licked it entirely, pal. Not till you face the facts about Joanna Sullivan."

"What facts?"

"She's no longer your sister-in-law. And you love her."

"Oh? What makes you so sure?"

"It's written all over your face. I might be an old man, Sullivan, but I'm not blind."

"All right. Say no more. So you can see right through me." Austin released a long sigh, then spread his hands wide. "I do love Joanna. I care for her more than I ever thought possible." He paused to give a rueful laugh. "Pretty sorry state for a confirmed bachelor like me, right?"

"Many a confirmed bachelor ended up changing his mind." Ted's eyes crinkled at the corners. "I ought to know. I was one of them."

"So what should I do?" Austin asked. He shoved his hands into his hip pockets, his shoulders slumped.

"Do you love her enough to marry her?"

"Yes—if she'll only have me."

"Then you'd better get busy, pal. Your time's running out."

***

Joanna parked the navy blue van, marked with the Southport Aquarium logo, onto a dirt strip below an embankment that was overgrown with wild grass.

Kerawk! Kerawk! Came the raucous sounds of the murres from the back of the van, where the seats had been temporarily taken out to make room for three dozen pens.

"Hold on, guys," Joanna said with a laugh. "It won't be long now."

Today she promised Ted she'd help with the release of the remaining birds. Since vehicles were limited, now that most of the volunteers had stopped coming, Trudy had suggested she take one of the vans that belonged to the aquarium.

Ted and Austin would soon be coming also in a pickup filled with grebes. The release site, Pomroy Point, was a well-protected estuary about sixty miles from Southport. State wildlife officials had determined it suitable because of its combined rocky shoreline, sandy beaches, and tidal mud flats, plus the probability that reoiling would not occur there.

Joanna flung open the van door and stepped outside. Hands on her hips, she stretched her back after the hour-long drive. A brisk wind teased her hair, whipping a strand across her forehead.

She exhaled slowly and thought, *this is it*. Tomorrow at this time Austin would most likely be gone. This time permanently. And as for her, she'd be back at the aquarium, glad to be there again, but nevertheless living out each lonely day at a time.

Whatever—she gave a quick shrug—it didn't matter anymore. Most likely she'd never see him again, especially after those hasty words she'd hurled at him when he'd returned to Anchorhold. The memory haunted her, leaving her filled with pain and regret. Now her cheeks burned as she realized anew he hadn't deserved that. At least, not all of it . . .

How was he to know she'd fallen in love with him? After all, she'd never told him. Without a doubt their kisses, their embraces, had meant nothing more to him than the heat of the moment. What else could she expect from a gorgeous man like Austin Sullivan, a man so vibrantly alive, a man so virile?

Kerawk! Kerawk! The murres' squawks sliced through her reverie, jolting her back.

"All right. I'm coming!" She grinned. The small pens weren't heavy. She anticipated little difficult in lifting them from the rear of the van and carrying them to the release site. So why wait for Ted and Austin to arrive? These birds were eager and restless. They were wonderful, wild things. Meant to be flying again. Meant to be free.

She carried one pen after the other over the narrow trail that bisected the knoll. Beyond lay the tide flat where beams of sunlight skittered off the glistening expanse of sand, mud, and gravel. To her right rose a rocky ridgeline, hugging the northernmost shore of the estuary. This would undoubtedly become the murres' next nesting spot, she thought.

Eyes moist with tears, her heart full, she released the first murre, then the next, and the next. Squawks punctuated the sound of flapping wings. At last the murres were all pressing skyward, brownish-black specks against the azure blue.

"Go, little ones," she said softly, one arm lifted in farewell. "You've fought hard for this. Now go."

Transfixed, she stood watching . . . for exactly how long, she wasn't sure. She longed to savor the moment forever, inscribe its significance in the most secret places of her soul.

"Jo." The sound was nearly a whisper.

Austin!

She turned to face him squarely, then looked around. "Where's Ted?" she asked, feigning nonchalance.

"I . . . I told him I wanted to come by myself. There weren't as many grebes as we first expected, so I said I could handle it. Actually I already released them at the other end of the bay." He swallowed hard as his eyes riveted on hers. "Bottom line is, I knew you'd be here alone too."

"I . . . I've turned loose the last of the murres," she said, blinking rapidly.

"I know. I was watching." His gaze was soulful and haunted.

"So . . . so I suppose you're almost ready to go again," she said in a rush.

"That's what we need to talk about."

"Oh?"

"I've been doing some heavy duty thinking about you . . . about me. I don't want to go back to California, Jo. But the only hope I could ever have of staying here is if I can *somehow* make you understand." She saw a muscle in his neck tighten. A hopeful look flashed in his dark eyes, then faded. "But I'm sure you're still so angry with me, so completely ticked off, there's no way."

"Understand what?"

"I realize now how badly I hurt you—especially during a time when you'd already been hurting. I never intended for that to happen. Please believe me. I've never meant anything more in my entire life."

"Oh, Austin . . . I do believe you." Her eyes shimmered with fresh tears. She bit her lower lip and swallowed hard, struggling to make sense of it all. So much had transpired these past several weeks.

"I'm not sure how I missed the signals, didn't realize what was happening between us," he hurried on. "Actually, when I stop to look back on it, I think I was in denial. Trying to convince myself this couldn't be happening, especially since you were Kyle's wife. But thanks to Ted, I've finally come to my senses. I know beyond all knowing, I love you. I need you. We're no longer wrong for each other. *We never were.*"

He caught her hand and gave it a hard squeeze. "I can only hope that I'm right in what I'm feeling—that somehow, some way, you love me too."

"Oh, yes. I *do* love you," she said, smiling up into his brown eyes. "Truth is, I've loved you from almost the first day you walked through my front door, though I was too confused then to have realized it. But I'm not confused any longer. And I'm sorry, Austin . . . sorry for all those horrible things I said."

"Apologies aren't necessary."

"Yes, they are. And you were right when you said I'd regret it later." She paused, then added, "Oh, how I regretted it."

"So you don't want me to go?"

"Of course not! I want you here. With me." She considered briefly, then asked. "But what about your job in San Francisco?"

"I think I'm ready to cash it in. I'm done with all the hassles. And if everything works out the way I hope it will, I'll be starting at Anchorhold the first of next month. Ted's made me an offer too good to pass up. He wants me to be his business partner."

"That's wonderful!"

"Yes, but ultimately, it all depends on you."

"Oh?"

"It depends on whether you love me enough to take a risk." He rested both hands on her shoulders. His touch seemed to sear right through her.

"Love you enough?" She spoke with so much intensity her voice trembled. "I love you because of who you are, Austin. Never in this entire world could there be another you. You're a man of integrity. A man who cares deeply enough not to make light of his promises." Flashing him a shy smile, she added, "A man whose very touch sends me to heights unknown."

He tucked back her hair and placed one hand on her nape, his thumb moving gently across her jaw. "And now I'd like to make a new promise—a promise to you, Jo. A pledge for all time before God and man." He hesitated before going on. "My darling . . . will you marry me? Be my wife?"

"Oh, yes!" She felt his hands drop to her waist as he pulled her close. Then his mouth covered hers with a long, slow kiss—a kiss that felt honest and right.

"Somehow . . . I feel as if Kyle is here with us," Austin murmured after they'd broken the contact.

"Yes, so do I. And he's smiling. I just know he is."

A moment later, arm-in-arm, they turned back to fetch the empty pens.

A cry sounded from overhead.

Together they looked up and smiled.

A murre drifted on a current of air, brilliant sunshine glinting off it wings.

The End

Don't miss out!

Visit the website below and you can sign up to receive emails whenever Sydell Lowell Voeller publishes a new book. There's no charge and no obligation.

https://books2read.com/r/B-A-KKZY-AOMNC

BOOKS 2 READ

Connecting independent readers to independent writers.

About the Author

Sydell Lowell Voeller grew up in Edmonds, Washington, and has lived in Forest Grove, Oregon for many years. Her family consists of a husband, two grown sons and their wives, and four grandchildren.

Sydell has been a violinist in semiprofessional orchestras, a registered nurse, and a writing instructor for the LongRidge Writer's Institute. Her interests include reading, camping, astronony, crafting, astronomy, and playing with her two cats.